TRANZLATY

Language is for everyone

语言属于每个人

The Call of Cthulhu

克蘇魯的呼喚

H.P. Lovecraft

H·P·洛夫克拉夫特

English

普通话

www.tranzlaty.com

The Horror Made of Clay
黏土造就的恐怖

There is one thing I find particularly merciful.

有一件事我觉得特别仁慈。

The inability of the human mind to correlate events.

人类思维无法将事件联系起来。

It's a blessing that we can't understand the world.

我们无法理解这个世界，这或许是一种幸运。

We live blissfully on a placid island of ignorance.

我们幸福地生活在一个平静的无知之岛上。

An island in the midst of black seas of infinity.

一座孤岛，矗立在无垠的黑色海洋之中。

And it was not meant that we should voyage far.

我们原本并不打算远航。

The sciences each strain in their own directions.

各个科学领域都朝着各自的方向发展。

But hitherto science's findings have harmed us little.

但迄今为止，科学发现对我们造成的伤害微乎其微。

But some day dissociated knowledge will be pieced together.

但总有一天，这些分散的知识会被拼凑起来。

Terrifying vistas of reality will open up to us.

我们将看到令人恐惧的现实景象。

And we will be left in a frightful vantage point.

我们将处于一个可怕的境地。

We will either go mad from the revelation we are given.

我们要么会因为所得到的启示而发疯。

Or we will flee from the deadly light that we will see.

否则我们将逃离我们将看到的致命光芒。

We will run from the knowledge we had always pursued.

我们将逃离我们一直以来所追求的知识。

And we will seek the peace and safety of a new dark age.

我们将寻求新黑暗时代的和平与安全。

Theosophists have guessed at the scale of the cosmos.

神智学家们曾对宇宙的尺度进行过推测。

Our world is but a transient incident in this cycle.

我们的世界只不过是这个循环中短暂的一瞬。

The human race plays but a little role in the universe.

人类在宇宙中扮演的角色微不足道。

The theosophists have hinted at strange methods of survival.

神智学家们暗示了一些奇特的生存方法。

But their suggestions would freeze a rational man's blood.

但他们的建议会让一个理性的人不寒而栗。

Only the optimism of their ideas hides the horror.

他们乐观的想法掩盖了其中的恐怖。

But it is not their ideas that chill me the most.

但最让我不寒而栗的并非他们的想法。

It is something else that fills me with terror.

还有另一件事让我感到恐惧。

The single glimpse of forbidden eons I have seen.

我所见到的，是禁忌时代的惊鸿一瞥。

When I think of what I saw my blood stands still.

每当我想起我所看到的景象，我的血液都停止了流动。

Restlessness plagues my dreams since that glimpse.

自从那一瞥之后，不安的情绪便一直困扰着我的梦境。

It came to me like all dreaded glimpses of truth.

它像所有令人恐惧的真相一样，突然出现在我的眼前。

An accidental piecing together of separated things.

意外地将分离的事物拼凑在一起。

An old newspaper item and the notes of a dead professor.

一份旧报纸文章和一位已故教授的笔记。

In a flash everything was pieced together before me.

转眼间，一切都清晰地呈现在我眼前。

I hope no one else will accomplish this terrible insight.

我希望不会再有人领悟到这种可怕的道理。

Certainly, if I live, I shall never help anyone to know it.

当然，如果我能活下来，我绝不会帮助任何人知道这件事。

I shall never knowingly supply a link in so hideous a chain.

我绝不会明知故犯地成为如此丑恶链条上的一环。

I think that the professor, too, intended to keep silent.

我认为教授也打算保持沉默。

He didn't mean to share the secrets that he knew.

他并非有意泄露自己所知道的秘密。

And I'm sure he would have destroyed his notes.

我相信他肯定会销毁他的笔记。

If he had not been seized by sudden and suspicious death.

如果他没有死于突如其来的可疑死亡的话。

***

My knowledge of the thing began in the winter of 1926-27.

我对这件事的了解始于 1926-27 年的冬天。

My great-uncle was the professor George Gammell Angell.

我的叔祖父是乔治·加梅尔·安吉尔教授。

He was the Professor Emeritus of Semitic languages.

他是闪米特语系荣誉退休教授。

He lectured in Brown University, Providence, Rhode Island.

他曾在罗德岛州普罗维登斯的布朗大学任教。

His death, at the age of ninety-two, triggered the event.

他去世时享年九十二岁，他的去世引发了这一事件。

He was widely known as an authority on ancient inscriptions.

他因精通古代铭文而广为人知。

Heads of prominent museums came to him for his expertise.

著名博物馆的馆长们都曾向他请教专业知识。

So his death was noticed by many within academic circles.

因此，他的去世引起了学术界许多人的关注。

Interest was intensified by the obscurity of his death.

他的死因不明反而加剧了人们的关注。

It occurred as he was disembarking from the Newport boat.

事情发生在他从纽波特号船上下来的时候。

Witnesses say a dark nautical-looking fellow had jostled him.

目击者称，一名肤色黝黑、穿着航海服的男子推了他一下。

After being stricken, he fell suddenly, witnesses say.

据目击者称，他中弹后突然倒地。

Physicians were unable to find any visible disorder.

医生未能发现任何可见的疾病。

After some perplexed debate they reached their conclusion.

经过一番令人困惑的讨论，他们最终得出结论。

"It must have been a lesion of the heart," they agreed.

"那一定是心脏的病变，"他们一致认为。

"After all, he was rather an elderly man," they added.

"毕竟，他年纪也比较大了，"他们补充道。

"the brisk ascent of the steep hill caused his end."

"他奋力攀登陡峭的山坡，结果丧命。"

At the time I saw no reason to dissent from this dictum.

当时我认为没有理由反对这条准则。

But latterly I am inclined to wonder about their conclusion.

但最近我开始对他们的结论产生怀疑。

And I do more than just wonder if they were right.

我不仅仅是想知道他们是否正确。

***

My grand-uncle died alone as a childless widower.

我的叔祖父去世时孤身一人，没有子女，是个鳏夫。

And so I became heir and executor to his possessions.

于是，我成了他财产的继承人和执行人。

So I was expected to go over his papers and writings.

所以，我需要审阅他的论文和著作。

I moved his entire set of files and boxes to my Boston home.

我把他的所有文件和箱子都搬到了我在波士顿的家中。

Much of the materials I collected will later be published.

我收集的大部分资料日后将会出版。

Many academics in his field took great interest in his work.

他所在领域的许多学者都对他的研究成果非常感兴趣。

The American archeological society relied on him greatly.

美国考古学会非常依赖他。

But there was one box which I found exceedingly puzzling.

但其中有一个盒子让我非常困惑。

I felt much averse from showing these files to other eyes.

我非常不愿意让别人看到这些文件。

The box had been locked, unlike the other boxes.

这个箱子被锁上了，与其他箱子不同。

And initially I found no key that would open this box.

一开始我找不到能打开这个盒子的钥匙。

But then the location of the key occurred to me.

但随后我突然想到了钥匙在哪儿。

The professor always carried a keyring in his pocket.

教授的口袋里总是装着一个钥匙扣。

It was indeed one of these keys that opened the box.

确实是这些钥匙中的一把打开了盒子。

But in the box was a still more closely locked barrier.

但盒子里还有一道更严密的屏障。

What could be the meaning of the queer bas-relief?

这幅奇特的浅浮雕可能意味着什么？

Various paper cuttings accompanied the bas-relief.

浮雕旁边还配有各种剪纸。

What did the disjointed jottings and ramblings allude to?

这些零散的随笔和随想究竟暗示了什么？

Had my uncle become credulous to superficial impostures?

我叔叔是不是轻信了肤浅的骗局？

Perhaps in his later years his criticalness thought slowed.

或许在他晚年，他的批判性思维有所减缓。

Someone had disturbed this old man's peace of mind.

有人打扰了这位老人的平静生活。

And so I resolved to locate the eccentric sculptor.

于是我决定找到这位古怪的雕塑家。

The man who set in motion my uncle's strange obsession.

引发我叔叔这种奇怪痴迷的就是这个人。

The bas-relief was roughly shaped like a rectangle.

浅浮雕大致呈长方形。

The rectangular shape was less than an inch thick.

这个长方形物体的厚度不到一英寸。

And the bas-relief was about five by six inches in area.

浅浮雕的面积约为五英寸乘六英寸。

It was obvious that the bas-relief was of modern origin.

很明显，这幅浅浮雕是近代的作品。

The designs, however, were far from modern in atmosphere.

然而，这些设计在氛围上与现代感相去甚远。

The inscriptions suggested a far older civilization.

铭文表明这里曾存在一个更为古老的文明。

The vagaries of cubism and futurism were many and wild.

立体主义和未来主义的风格变化多端、天马行空。

But normally such patterns fail to produce regularity.

但通常情况下，这种模式无法产生规律性。

The cryptic regularity which lurks in prehistoric writing.

史前文字中隐藏的神秘规律。

This regularity was certainly present in the bas-relief.

这种规律性在浅浮雕中确实存在。

I was certain the inscriptions represented a writing system.

我确信这些铭文代表了一种文字系统。

I had some familiarity with the papers of my uncle.

我对叔叔的文件略有了解。

And I had looked through all of his collections and works.

我翻阅过他的所有收藏和作品。

But I failed to find any writing that was similar.

但我没能找到任何类似的文章。

I could not geographically place this alphabet in any way.

我完全无法确定这套字母表的地理位置。

Nor could I guess from what time this writing came from.

我无法判断这篇文章的写作时间。

Above these apparent hieroglyphics there was a figure.

在这些看似象形文字的上方，有一个图案。

The figure was evidently only of pictorial intent.

该人物显然仅具绘画用途。

The impressionism of the picture added to the mystery.

画作的印象派风格更增添了神秘感。

No clear idea of the creature's nature could be discerned.

人们无法清楚地了解这种生物的性质。

The creature seemed to be a monster, of some sort.

那生物看起来像某种怪物。

Or the symbol represented a monster, of some sort.

或者，这个符号代表某种怪物。

Only a diseased mind could conceive of such a form.

只有病态的心灵才能构想出这样的形式。

My imagination yielded different pictures simultaneously.

我的想象力同时浮现出不同的画面。

But my imagination may also be somewhat extravagant.

但我的想象力可能也有些过于丰富了。

An octopus, a dragon, and also a human caricature.

一只章鱼、一条龙，还有一个人物漫画形象。

I shall try not be unfaithful to the spirit of the thing.

我将尽量不违背事情的初衷。

A pulpy, tentacled head surmounted a scaly body.

一个肉乎乎的、长着触手的头部，长在一个布满鳞片的身
体上。

Rudimentary wings protruded from the grotesque shape.
从怪异的形状中伸出退化的翅膀。

But the shape of the monster wasn't even the worst part.
但怪物的外形还不是最糟糕的部分。

The background of the picture was even more frightening.
照片的背景更加恐怖。

The scenery had a vague suggestion of another civilization.
眼前的景色隐约透露出另一种文明的气息。

Cyclopean architecture from a forgotten part of the world.
来自世界某个被遗忘角落的巨型建筑。

***

Only some notes and press cuttings accompanied the oddity.
只有一些笔记和剪报与这件怪事相伴。

The press cuttings seemed to be only vaguely related.
这些剪报似乎只有一些模糊的关联。

The hand written notes were all from my uncle.
这些手写便条都是我叔叔写的。

But his notes made no pretense to any literary style.
但他的笔记丝毫没有追求任何文学风格。

There was no ordering mechanism to any of the papers.
所有论文都没有排序机制。

Although there seemed to be a master document to the
notes.
虽然笔记似乎有一个总文档。

This document was ascribed to the cult of Cthulhu

这份文件被认为是克苏鲁教的文献。

The word's letters had been painstakingly written out.

这个词的每个字母都是经过精心拼写出来的。

There should be no erroneous reading of the unheard of word.

对于从未听过的词语，不应该有误读。

This Cthulhu manuscript was divided into two sections;

这部克苏鲁手稿分为两部分；

The first manuscript was titled the following:

第一份手稿的标题如下：

"1925 - Dream and Dream Work of H. A. Wilcox"

1925年——H. A. 威尔科克斯的梦与梦的工作

"7 Thomas St., Providence, Road Island"

"罗德岛普罗维登斯托马斯街7号"

And the second manuscript was titled the following:

第二份手稿的标题如下：

"Narrative of Inspector John R. Legrasse"

《约翰·R·勒格拉斯探长叙述》

"121 Bienville St., New Orleans, 1908 Meetings."

新奥尔良比恩维尔街121号，1908年会议

"Notes on Same, & Prof. Webb's account of events"

"关于萨姆的笔记，以及韦伯教授对事件的描述"

The other manuscript papers were all brief notes.

其他手稿都是简短的笔记。

Some manuscripts described the queer dreams of different persons.

有些手稿描述了不同人的奇异梦境。

Some manuscripts cited from theosophical books and magazines.

部分手稿引自神智学书籍和杂志。

Notably, most of these citations were from W. Scott-Eliott.

值得注意的是，这些引文大多来自 W. 斯科特-埃利奥特。

Mainly the notes referenced Atlantis and the Lost Lemuria.

笔记主要提到了亚特兰蒂斯和失落的利莫里亚。

The other notes commented on long-surviving secret societies.

其他笔记评论了长期存在的秘密社团。

Hidden cults that may or may not still exist somewhere.

可能仍然存在于某些地方的隐秘邪教组织。

Two books seemed to provide most of the information;

两本书似乎提供了大部分信息；

Miss Murray's Witch-Cult in Western Europe.

穆雷小姐在西欧的女巫崇拜。

This book thoroughly detailed Mythological sources.

这本书详尽地介绍了神话来源。

And Frazer's Golden Bough provided anthropological sources.

弗雷泽的《金枝》提供了人类学方面的资料。

***

The cuttings largely alluded to outré mental illnesses.

这些剪报大多影射了离奇的精神疾病。

Outbreaks of group folly and mania in the spring of 1925.

1925年春季爆发群体愚行和狂热事件。

The first half of the manuscript told a very peculiar tale.

手稿的前半部分讲述了一个非常奇特的故事。

1925, the 1st of March, a thin dark young man came to my uncle.

1925年3月1日，一个瘦削黝黑的年轻男子来到我叔叔家。

The manuscript describes his neurotic and excited aspect.

手稿描述了他神经质和易怒的一面。

And he bore with him the strange bas-relief.

他带着那奇特的浅浮雕。

At that time the bas-relief was exceedingly damp and fresh.

当时，浮雕非常潮湿，而且很新鲜。

His card bore the name of Henry Anthony Wilcox.

他的名片上写着亨利·安东尼·威尔科克斯的名字。

And my uncle had slightly recognized who he was.

我叔叔隐约认出了他是谁。

He was the youngest son of an excellent family.

他是出身名门的幼子。

Latterly he had been studying sculpture at Rhode Island.

他后来在罗德岛学习雕塑。

He lived alone at the Fleur-de-Lys Building.

他独自一人住在百合花大厦。

His residences were near the university.

他的住所靠近大学。

Wilcox was a precocious youth of known genius.

威尔科克斯是一位早慧的天才少年。

But he was also known for his great eccentricity.

但他同时也以其古怪的性格而闻名。

From childhood he had excited the attention of others.

他从小就引人注目。

He told of strange stories no one had told him about.

他讲述了一些别人从未告诉过他的奇怪故事。

And he was in the habit of relating strange dreams.

他经常讲述一些奇怪的梦境。

He described himself as "psychically hypersensitive".

他形容自己是"精神高度敏感者"。
But those around him had other descriptions for him.
但他身边的人对他却有不同的评价。
They were staid folk of the ancient commercial city.
他们是这座古老商业城市里性格沉稳的居民。
And they dismissed him as merely strange and "queer".
他们只觉得他古怪、"另类"。
And so he never mingled much with his kind.
因此，他很少与同类交往。
And he had dropped gradually from social visibility.
他逐渐淡出了社会公众视野。
Now he is known only to a small group of esthetes.
现在只有一小群审美家知道他。
And those who knew him came mostly from other towns.
认识他的人大多来自其他城镇。
Even the Providence art club had found him quite hopeless.
就连普罗维登斯艺术俱乐部都觉得他完全没救了。
Of course they were anxious to preserve their conservatism.
他们当然渴望维护自己的保守主义。

***

The professor's manuscript continued to describe the visit.
教授的手稿继续描述了这次访问。
The sculptor abruptly asked for his host's archeological
knowledge.
雕塑家突然询问主人的考古知识。
He wanted him to identify the hieroglyphics on the bas-
relief.

他想让他辨认浅浮雕上的象形文字。

He spoke in a dreamy and rather stilted manner.

他说话的语气梦幻而略显生硬。

His speech suggested pose and alienated sympathy.

他的演讲显得矫揉造作，令人反感。

And my uncle showed some sharpness in his reply.

我叔叔的回答却颇为犀利。

Because the bas-relief was still conspicuously freshness.

因为浮雕仍然非常新鲜。

So there was no need for any kinship with archeology.

所以它与考古学没有任何关联。

Young Wilcox's rejoinder was of a fantastically poetic cast.

年轻的威尔科克斯的回应极富诗意。

My uncle must have been impressed with the reply.

我叔叔一定对这个答复印象深刻。

And he recorded the reply of Wilcox verbatim.

他一字不差地记录了威尔科克斯的答复。

"The bas-relief is indeed still conspicuously fresh."

“这幅浅浮雕确实依然非常清晰。”

"Because I made this bas-relief last night, after a dream."

“因为我昨晚做梦后创作了这个浅浮雕。”

"A dream of strange cities and stranger people."

“一个关于陌生城市和陌生人的梦。”

"And dreams are older than brooding Tyros."

“而梦想比忧郁的泰罗斯还要古老。”

"Dreams are older than the contemplative Sphinx."

“梦想比沉思的斯芬克斯还要古老。”

"And dreams are older than the garden-girdled Babylon."

“而梦想比被花园环绕的巴比伦还要古老。”

This type of speech turned out to be characteristic of him.

这种演讲风格后来被证明是他的特色。

It was then that he began that rambling tale.

就在那时，他开始讲述那个冗长的故事。

The tale which suddenly played upon a sleeping memory.

这个故事突然唤醒了沉睡的记忆。

The tale that won the fevered interest of my uncle.

这个故事引起了我叔叔的极大兴趣。

***

There had been a slight earthquake tremor the night before.

前一天晚上曾发生过轻微的地震。

The most considerable tremor New England had felt for some years.

这是新英格兰地区多年来感受到的最强烈的地震。

Wilcox's imagination had been keenly affected by the earthquake.

地震对威尔科克斯的想象力产生了深刻的影响。

He had had an unprecedented dream of great Cyclopean cities.

他做了一个前所未有的梦，梦见了巨大的独眼巨人般的城市。

He dreamed of Titan blocks and sky-flung monoliths.

他梦见了泰坦巨石和高耸入云的巨石。

All the architecture was dripping with green ooze.

所有建筑都滴着绿色的黏液。

And his dreams were sinister with latent horror.

他的梦境阴森恐怖，潜藏着可怕的预兆。

Hieroglyphics had covered the walls and pillars.

墙壁和柱子上都刻满了象形文字。

From somewhere underneath there came a sound.

下方某处传来一声响动。

The sound was of a voice, but it was not a voice.

那声音像是人声，但又不是人声。

A chaotic sensation which only fancy could transmute into sound.

一种混乱的感觉，只有想象力才能将其转化为声音。

He attempted to say the almost unpronounceable word.

他试图说出那个几乎无法发音的词。

A jumble of unlikely letters; "Cthulhu fhtagn".

一串不太可能的字母；“克苏鲁复苏”。

This verbal jumble was the key to my uncle's recollection.

这番语无伦次的话语是我叔叔回忆的关键。

This strange sound excited and disturbed Professor Angell.

这种奇怪的声音让安吉尔教授既兴奋又不安。

He questioned the sculptor with scientific minuteness.

他以科学的严谨态度向雕塑家提问。

He studied the bas-relief with almost frantic intensity.

他近乎疯狂地仔细研究着这幅浅浮雕。

My uncle blamed his old age, Wilcox afterward said.

威尔科克斯后来表示，我叔叔把这归咎于自己年老体衰。

In his younger days he would have recognized the hieroglyphics.

年轻的时候他应该能认出这些象形文字。

The pictorial design wouldn't have puzzled his sharper mind.

如此精明的设计，难不倒他敏锐的头脑。

Many of his questions seemed highly out of place to his visitor.

他的许多问题对于他的访客来说似乎都非常不合适。

He tried to connect him to strange mythological cults.

他试图将他与一些奇怪的神话教派联系起来。

He tried to get him to admit affiliation to secret societies.

他试图让他承认自己与秘密社团有关联。

My uncle even promised to keep his visitor's secret.

我叔叔甚至答应保守访客的秘密。

"Are you not part of a widespread mystical group?"

"你是不是某个庞大的神秘组织的成员？"

"Are you not a member of a paganly religious body?"

"你不是某个异教宗教团体的成员吗？"

Eventually he became convinced the sculptor wasn't a member.

最终他确信这位雕塑家不是会员。

He was indeed ignorant of any cult or system of cryptic lore.

他对任何邪教或神秘传说体系确实一无所知。

He besieged his visitor with demands for future reports of dreams.

他纠缠着来访者，要求他汇报未来的梦境。

This strange request bore regular and interesting fruit.

这个奇怪的要求结出了定期且有趣的果实。

***

After the first interview the manuscript records daily calls.

第一次采访结束后，稿件记录了每天的通话内容。

He related startling fragments of nocturnal imagery.

他讲述了一些令人震惊的夜间景象片段。

There were always the same themes in his dreams.

他的梦境总是围绕着同样的主题。

A terrible Cyclopean vista of dark and dripping stone.

一片可怕的、如同巨石般黑暗且滴水的景象。

A subterranean voice or intelligence shouting monotonously.

地下传来单调的呼喊声或智慧之声。

Two sounds seemed to repeat themselves in his dreams.

他的梦里似乎反复出现两种声音。

But these sounds were as enigmatic as the other sounds.

但这些声音和其他声音一样神秘莫测。

The sounds can only be rendered by the letters "Cthulhu" and "R'lyeh".

这些声音只能用字母"克苏鲁"和"瑞莱耶"来表达。

On March 23rd, the manuscript continued, Wilcox failed to come.

手稿继续写道，3月23日，威尔科克斯没有来。

My uncle made inquiries at the quarters of his whereabouts.

我叔叔向他的住处打听他的下落。

That night he had been stricken with an obscure sort of fever.

那天晚上他得了一种不知名的发烧病。

And he was taken to the home of his family in Waterman Street.

然后他被送回了位于沃特曼街的家中。

That night he had cried out in one of his dreams.

那天晚上，他在梦中发出了一声哭喊。

His cries aroused several other artists in the building.

他的喊叫声惊动了楼里的其他几位艺术家。

And he was between alternations of unconsciousness and delirium.

他时而昏迷，时而谵妄。

My uncle at once telephoned the family of Wilcox.

我叔叔立即打电话给威尔科克斯一家。

And from that time forward he kept close watch of the case.

从那时起，他就密切关注着这个案子。

He called often at the Thayer Street office of Dr. Tobey.

他经常去托比医生位于泰耶街的办公室拜访。

Dr. Tobey was in charge of the patient's condition.

托比医生负责该病人的病情。

The youth's febrile mind was dwelling on strange things.

少年躁动不安，满脑子都是些奇怪的事情。

The doctor shuddered now and then as he spoke of the dreams.

医生在谈到那些梦境时，不时会感到一阵颤抖。

The dreams repeated a lot of the earlier themes.

这些梦境重复出现了很多之前出现过的主题。

But now his dreams made mention of something new.

但现在他的梦境中出现了新的内容。

A gigantic thing "a miles high" which walked, or lumbered about.

一个"高达数英里"的庞然大物，它会行走，或者蹒跚而行。

He at no time fully described this object in any detail.

他始终没有对这个物体进行任何详细的描述。

But Dr. Tobey relayed the frantic words of his patient.

但托比医生转述了他病人惊慌失措的话。

And the professor became increasingly certain of what it was.

教授越来越确信那是什么。

The nameless monstrosity he had sought to depict in his sculpture.

他试图在雕塑中描绘的那个无名怪物。

The doctor had mentioned the bas-relief he had made.

医生曾提到过他制作的浅浮雕。

This mention preludes the young man's subsidence into lethargy.

这句话预示着这个年轻人即将陷入昏昏欲睡的状态。

His temperature, oddly enough, was not greatly above normal.

奇怪的是，他的体温并没有比正常值高出多少。

But his general condition suggested he was in a fever.

但他的整体状况表明他发烧了。

A fever, as opposed to being in the grasp of a mental disorder.

发烧，而不是患有精神疾病。

***

On April 2nd at about 3 p.m. the fever came to an end.

4月2日下午3点左右，烧退了。

Every trace of Wilcox's malady suddenly ceased.

威尔科克斯的所有病症突然消失了。

He sat upright in bed as if waking up from regular sleep.

他像刚从睡梦中醒来一样，在床上坐了起来。

He was astonished to find himself at his parents' home.

他惊讶地发现自己身处父母家中。

And he was completely ignorant of what had happened.

他对发生的事情完全一无所知。

Neither dream nor reality had made an impression on his mind.

梦境和现实都没能给他留下任何印象。

Dr. Tobey pronounced him fit to be dismissed from his care.

托比医生宣布他身体状况良好，可以出院了。

And he returned to his quarters three days later.

三天后，他返回了自己的住处。

But to Professor Angell he was of no further assistance.

但他对安吉尔教授来说已无任何帮助。

All traces of strange dreaming had vanished with his recovery.

随着他的康复，所有奇怪的梦境痕迹都消失了。

For a week he recounted irrelevant and thoroughly usual visions.

整整一周，他都在讲述一些无关紧要且极其普通的幻象。

And my uncle kept no further record of his night-thoughts.

我的叔叔再也没有记录过他的夜间想法。

At this point the first part of the manuscript ended.

至此，手稿的第一部分就结束了。

But my research was still anything but concluded.

但我的研究远未结束。

References to scattered notes helped piece things together.

参考零散的笔记，我们才得以将事情拼凑起来。

And there was more than enough material for thought.

而且，可供思考的素材也绰绰有余。

My distrust of the artist had still not subsided.

我对这位艺术家的不信任感依然没有消退。

But this was largely a result of my ingrained skepticism.

但这很大程度上是由于我根深蒂固的怀疑主义造成的。

The notes described the dreams of various persons.

笔记中描述了不同人的梦境。

These dreams all occurred while young Wilcox was in his fever.

这些梦境都是在小威尔科克斯发烧期间发生的。

My uncle, it seems, wasted no time in collecting the data.

看来，我叔叔很快就收集到了数据。

He had quickly instituted a prodigiously far-flung body of inquiries.

他迅速启动了一项规模庞大、涉及面极广的调查。

Any friend that didn't show impertinence he questioned.

任何没有表现出无礼的朋友，他都会质疑。

He requested from them nightly reports of their dreams.

他要求他们每晚汇报梦境。

And he asked if they had had any notable visions of late.

他问他们最近是否有什么特别的异象。

The reception of his request seems to have been varied.

他的请求似乎得到了不同的回应。

But there was certainly no shortage in replies.

但回复的数量绝对不少。

No ordinary man could have handled the replies alone.

普通人不可能独自处理这些回复。

The original correspondences were not preserved.

原始信件并未保存下来。

But his notes formed a thorough and significant digest.

但他的笔记构成了一份全面而重要的摘要。

***

Initially he had approached average people in society.

起初，他接触的是社会上的普通人。

New England's traditional "salt of the earth".

新英格兰传统的"朴实无华之人"。

But this group gave an almost completely negative result.

但该组的结果几乎完全为阴性。

Though there were some exceptions to this group too.

当然，这个群体中也有一些例外。

Scattered cases of uneasy but formless nocturnal impressions.

零星出现的不安但模糊的夜间印象。

Their reports were always between March 23rd and April 2nd.

他们的报告总是在3月23日至4月2日之间。

This aligned with the same period of young Wilcox's delirium.

这与年轻的威尔科克斯出现谵妄症状的时期相吻合。

Men of science had been only a little more affected.

科学家受到的影响也只是略大一些而已。

Though four cases of vague description were of interest.

虽然有四个描述模糊的案例，但仍然值得关注。

They had had fugitive glimpses of strange landscapes.

他们曾匆匆瞥见过一些奇异的景色。

And in one case a dread of something abnormal was mentioned.

其中一例提到了对某种异常情况的恐惧。

It was from the artists and poets that the pertinent answers came.

相关的答案都来自艺术家和诗人。

It is a blessing no one had been able to compare notes.

幸好之前没有人能够交流信息。

Panic would have broken loose had they shared their visions.

如果他们分享了自己的幻象，恐慌就会爆发。

This, however, did not dispel my ingrained skepticism.

然而，这并没有消除我根深蒂固的怀疑。

Others might have come to mythical conclusions much quicker.

其他人或许会更快地得出神话般的结论。

But the original letters were lacking from the notes.

但笔记中缺少了原信。

I half suspected the compiler of having asked leading questions.

我当时隐隐怀疑编译器问了一些引导性问题。

Or perhaps the correspondences weren't entirely original.

或许这些信件并非完全原创。

Perhaps my uncle had resolved to confirm Wilcox's dreams.

或许我叔叔决心要实现威尔科克斯的梦想。

That is why I continued to feel suspicious of the sculptor.

这就是我一直对这位雕塑家抱有怀疑的原因。

Perhaps he was still cognizant of my uncle's old data.

或许他仍然记得我叔叔以前的数据。

Perhaps he had been imposing on the veteran scientist.

或许他是在对这位资深科学家颐指气使。

Nonetheless, the corroborating data had to be investigated.

然而，还需要对佐证数据进行调查。

***

The responses from the esthetes told a disturbing tale.

美学家们的反应讲述了一个令人不安的故事。

From February 28th to April 2nd their dreams aligned.

从2月28日至4月2日，他们的梦想不谋而合。

And a large proportion of them had dreamed very bizarre things.

他们当中很大一部分人都做过非常离奇的梦。

The timing of the intensity of their dreams was also of interest.

他们梦境的强度出现的时间也值得关注。

The period of the sculptor's delirium marked a highpoint.

雕塑家精神错乱的时期标志着他创作生涯的高峰期。

The intensity of their dreams were immeasurably the stronger.

他们的梦境强度要强得多。

Over a quarter reported unfamiliar and unpronounceable sounds.

超过四分之一的人表示听到了不熟悉且无法发音的声音。

Noises not dissimilar to what Wilcox had also described.

与威尔科克斯描述的声音非常相似。

Some described highly elaborate and impossible architecture.

有些人描述了极其复杂且不可能实现的建筑。

And some of the dreamers confessed to an acute fear.

有些做梦者坦言自己内心充满恐惧。

Like Wilcox, they had seen some gigantic nameless thing.

和威尔科克斯一样，他们也看到了某种巨大的、没有名字的东西。

One case, which the note describes with emphasis, was very sad.

其中一个案例非常令人悲伤，笔记中着重描述了这个案例。

The subject was a widely known architect of the region.

被传主是当地一位广为人知的建筑师。

He too had leanings toward theosophy and occultism.

他也对神智学和神秘学感兴趣。

This man went violently insane on March the 22nd.

3月22日，这名男子突然精神失常。

The exact same date of young Wilcox's seizure.

与小威尔科克斯癫痫发作的日期完全相同。

He expired several months later, after incessant screaming.

几个月后，他在持续不断的尖叫声中死去。

He begged to be saved from some escaped denizen of hell.

他恳求被救，免遭某个从地狱逃脱的恶魔的毒手。

Regrettably, my uncle did not refer to these cases by name.

遗憾的是，我叔叔没有提及这些案件的名称。

Instead, all studies were given nothing more than a number.

相反，所有研究都只被赋予了一个数字。

This way I was limited in attempting any personal investigation.

这样一来，我就无法进行任何个人调查了。

And corroborating the evidence further was demanding.

进一步证实这些证据非常困难。

But finally I did succeed in tracing down some cases.

但最终我还是成功追踪到了一些案件。

I should have trusted the notes from my uncle.

我真应该相信我叔叔留下的字条。

They reported their dreams true to their reports.

他们如实报告了他们的梦境。

I have often wondered what they thought the questioning meant.

我常常想知道，他们认为这些问题意味着什么。

It is for the best that no explanation shall ever reach them.

最好永远不要让他们听到任何解释。

***

As I have mentioned, my uncle also collected press clippings.

正如我之前提到的，我叔叔也收集剪报。

These press clippings corresponded to the dates in question.

这些剪报与所涉日期相符。

The sources were scattered throughout the globe.

这些资源分散在全球各地。

Professor Angell must have employed a cutting bureau.

安吉尔教授肯定雇佣了一个裁缝。

Because the number of extracts was tremendous.

因为提取物的数量非常庞大。

There was a parallel to this part of his research.

他的研究与此部分有相似之处。

Cases of panic, mania, and eccentricity.

恐慌症、躁狂症和怪异行为病例。

One case was a nocturnal suicide in London.

其中一起案件是发生在伦敦的夜间自杀事件。

A lone sleeper had leaped from a window after a shocking cry.

一声惊叫后，一名独自睡觉的男子从窗户跳了出去。

A rambling letter to the editor of a paper in South America.

一封写给南美某报纸编辑的冗长信件。

A fanatic deduces a dire future from visions he had had.

一个狂热分子根据他所做的幻象推断出一个可怕的未来。

A dispatch from California describes a theosophist colony.

一份来自加利福尼亚的报道描述了一个神智学会的聚居地
。

They donned white robes en masse for some "glorious fulfilment".

他们集体穿上白色长袍，以求获得某种"光荣的满足"。

Although that "glorious fulfilment" never arose.

虽然那种"辉煌的实现"从未发生。

There seems to be serious unrest from the natives in India.

印度当地民众似乎出现了严重的骚乱。

Voodoo orgies multiplied in Haiti.

海地巫毒教狂欢活动激增。

African outposts report ominous mutterings.

非洲前哨站传来不祥的低语声。

American officers in the Philippines find certain tribes bothersome.

驻菲律宾的美国军官觉得某些部落很麻烦。

New York policemen are mobbed by hysterical Levantines.

纽约警察被歇斯底里的黎凡特人围攻。

This occurred exactly on the night of March 22-23.

这件事恰好发生在3月22日至23日夜间。

The west of Ireland, too, was full of wild rumor and legendry.

爱尔兰西部也充满了各种离奇的谣言和传说。

A fantastic painter named Ardois-Bonnot made the news in France.

一位名叫阿尔杜瓦-博诺的杰出画家在法国上了新闻。

He hung a blasphemous dream landscape in the Paris spring salon.

他在巴黎春季沙龙里挂了一幅亵渎神明的梦幻风景画。

The recorded troubles in insane asylums were immeasurable.

精神病院发生的种种问题数不胜数。

A miracle must have kept the medical fraternities unsuspecting.

一定是奇迹发生了，医学界才没有察觉到这一切。

But they never noted the strange parallelisms of the cases.

但他们从未注意到这些案件之间奇怪的相似之处。

Else they too would have come to mystified conclusions.

否则，他们也会得出令人费解的结论。

I must confess these were indeed a set of weird paper cuttings.

我必须承认，这些确实是一组奇特的剪纸作品。

My uncle had put forward a convincing argument.

我叔叔提出了一个令人信服的论点。

I can't explain how I set the evidence aside.

我无法解释我为什么把证据放在一边。

But my callous rationalism took the upper hand.

但我冷酷的理性最终占据了上风。

And I was still suspicious of the young sculptor, Wilcox.

我仍然对年轻的雕塑家威尔科克斯抱有怀疑。

He must have known of the older matters mentioned by the professor.

他肯定知道教授提到的那些旧事。

The Tale of Inspecter Legrasse
勒格拉斯探长的故事

Let me turn your attention away from the young sculptor.

让我把你们的注意力从这位年轻的雕塑家身上转移开来。

And let us focus on the second half of the manuscript.

接下来，让我们重点关注稿件的后半部分。

A few dreams alone would not have been so significant.

仅仅几个梦境并不会如此意义重大。

The bas-relief could have been dismissed as a hoax.

这幅浅浮雕原本可能被认为是骗局。

But my uncle had previously been primed to take interest.

但我叔叔之前就已经对此产生了兴趣。

Wilcox's dream seemed to have a link to past events.

威尔科克斯的梦似乎与过去的事件有关。

It wasn't the first time that he had heard that word.

这并非他第一次听到这个词。

The ominous syllables perhaps written as "Cthulhu".

这些不祥的音节或许可以写成“克苏鲁”。

He had seen and heard of similar descriptions before.

他以前见过或听说过类似的描述。

The hellish outlines of the nameless monstrosity.

那无名怪物的恐怖轮廓。

He had previously puzzled over the same hieroglyphics.

他之前也曾对同样的象形文字感到困惑。

All this produced a horrible connection of events.

这一切最终导致了一系列可怕的事件。

It is no wonder he pursued young Wilcox with queries.

难怪他会追问年轻的威尔科克斯。

And we must not be surprised he interrogated Wilcox so.

我们不应该对他如此审问威尔科克斯感到惊讶。

This earlier experience had come in the year of 1908.

此前的这段经历发生在1908年。

Seventeen years before Wilcox came to my great-uncle.

威尔科克斯来到我叔祖父家之前十七年。

The archeological society were meeting in St. Louis.

考古学会正在圣路易斯举行会议。

Professor Angell had a prominent part in the deliberations.

安吉尔教授在讨论中发挥了重要作用。

His responsibilities befitted one of his authority.

他的职责与他的职权相符。

He was one of the first to be approached by several outsiders.

他是最早被几位外来者接触的人之一。

They took advantage of the convocation to offer questions.

他们利用这次集会的机会提出了问题。

They hoped for correct answering from an expert.

他们希望得到专家的正确答案。

They each had very peculiar types of problems.

他们各自遇到的问题都非常特殊。

And they required very different types of solutions.

他们需要的解决方案截然不同。

The chief of these was a common-looking middle-aged man.

这些人中的首领是一位相貌平平的中年男子。

And he quickly became the meeting's focus of interest.

他很快就成了会议的焦点。

***

He had traveled to St. Louis all the way from New Orleans.

他从新奥尔良一路来到圣路易斯。

He had come to the meeting for special information.

他来参加会议是为了获取一些特殊信息。

Knowledge that could not be unobtained from local source.

从当地来源无法获得的知识。

His name was John Raymond Legrasse, police inspector.

他的名字叫约翰·雷蒙德·勒格拉斯，是一名警督。

He bore with him the mysterious subject of his inquiries.

他带着这份神秘的探究欲去探究。

A grotesque and apparently very ancient stone statuette.

一尊造型怪诞且显然非常古老的石雕像。

A statuette whose origin no one had been able to determine.

一尊来历不明的小雕像。

But don't assume Inspector Legrasse was an archeologist.

但不要以为勒格拉斯探长是考古学家。

He had very little interest in archeology, nor mythology.

他对考古学和神话学都没什么兴趣。

His wish for enlightenment had rather different motivations.

他渴望获得启迪的动机却截然不同。

He was prompted to come by purely professional considerations.

他此行完全是出于职业考虑。

The statuette had been captured as part of a police raid.

这尊雕像是在一次警方突袭行动中缴获的。

Although whether it was even a statuette wasn't determined.

尽管尚无法确定它是否真的是一座小雕像。

It could also have been an idol, magic fetish, or charm.

它也可能是一个偶像、魔法护身符或护身符。

Whatever it was, it had been captured some months previously.

无论那是什么，都是几个月前捕获的。

A meeting was being held in the wooded swamps of New Orleans.

会议在新奥尔良的林木茂密的沼泽地带举行。

The police had been tipped of about a supposed voodoo meeting.

警方此前接到线报，称有人要举行巫毒仪式。

Strange and hideous rites connected with the voodoo circle.

与巫毒教相关的怪异而可怕的仪式。

The police could not but realize what they had stumbled on.

警方不得不意识到他们发现了什么。

A dark cult previously totally unknown to the authorities.

一个此前当局完全不知情的黑暗邪教组织。

Infinitely more sinister than what an outsider could expect.

比外人所能想象的要险恶得多。

More diabolic than the blackest of the African voodoo circles.

比非洲最邪恶的巫毒教圈子还要邪恶。

Unbelievable tales were extorted from the captured cult members.

从被俘的邪教成员口中逼供出了令人难以置信的故事。

But nothing of the relic's origin could be discovered.

但是，关于这件文物的来源，却一无所获。

Hence the anxiety of the police for any antiquarian lore.

因此，警方对任何古籍轶事都感到焦虑。

Ancient mythology might explain the frightful symbol.

古代神话或许可以解释这个可怕的符号。

Deeper knowledge could perhaps track the fountain-head.

更深入的了解或许可以追溯到源头。

Inspector Legrasse was not prepared for the excitement he created.

勒格拉斯探长没想到自己会引起如此大的轰动。

One sight of the mysterious object was all that was required.

只需看一眼那个神秘物体就足够了。

The assembled men of science were filled with curiosity.

聚集在一起的科学家们充满了好奇。

They lost no time in crowding closely around the inspector.

他们立即围拢在检查员周围。

And they all tried to get the best look at the diminutive figure.

他们都想看清这个矮小的身影。

***

The genuinely abysmal antiquity inspired wild imagination.

古代那段极其悲惨的历史激发了人们天马行空的想象力。

The strangeness hinted so potently at unopened and archaic vistas.

这种奇异感强烈地暗示着尚未开启的古老景象。

No recognized school of sculpture had animated this terrible object.

没有哪个公认的雕塑流派赋予这件可怕的物体以生命。

Yet centuries seemed recorded in the dim and greenish surface.

然而，昏暗泛绿的表面上似乎记录了几个世纪的历史。

Perhaps thousands of years were hidden in this unplaceable stone.

或许这块无法归类的石头里隐藏着数千年的历史。

The figurine was finally passed slowly from man to man.

这尊雕像最终在人与人之间慢慢地流传下去。

Each scientist carefully studied the strange markings of the stone.

每位科学家都仔细研究了石头上的奇特纹路。

The work was between seven and eight inches in height.

这件作品高约七到八英寸。

And the exquisite artistic workmanship must be noted.

此外，其精湛的艺术工艺也值得称道。

The carvings represented a monster of vaguely anthropoid outline.

这些雕刻描绘了一个轮廓模糊、类似人形的怪物。

On the face of the octopus-esque head was a mass of feelers.

章鱼状的头部表面布满了触须。

Prodigious claws on hind and fore feet protruded from the body.

后脚和前脚上长着巨大的爪子，从身体上突出。

The bloated corpulence had a rubbery looking quality to it.

肿胀的体液看起来像橡胶一样。

And from behind the rubbery body came out two narrow wings.

从橡胶般的身体后面伸出了两只狭长的翅膀。

It would be instinctual to think of this thing as fearsome.

人们本能地会觉得这东西很可怕。

There was an unnatural malignancy to the aura of the creature.

这生物身上散发着一种不自然的邪恶气息。

The gargantuan squatted evilly on a rectangular block.

那个庞然大物邪恶地蹲在一个长方形的方块上。

The pedestal it was on was covered with undecipherable characters.

它所处的基座上刻满了无法辨认的文字。

The tips of the wings touched the back edge of the block.

翅膀的尖端触碰到了木块的后边缘。

The creature was sitting on the middle of the giant block.

那生物正坐在巨石的中央。

Its legs were doubled up under its monstrous body.

它的双腿蜷缩在它庞大的身躯之下。

The long, curved claws gripped the front edge of the cliff.

长长的弯曲爪子紧紧抓住悬崖的前缘。

The cephalopod head was bent forward, observing its kingdom.

头足类动物的头部向前弯曲，观察着它的王国。

The ends of the facial feelers brushed the backs of huge forepaws.

面部触须的末端拂过巨大的前爪背部。

And the forepaws clasped the croucher's elevated knees.

前爪紧紧抓住蹲伏者抬起的膝盖。

The appearance of the grotesque scene was abnormally lifelike.

这幅怪诞的画面看起来异常逼真。

But this lifelike quality only added a subtle reason to be more fearful.

但这种栩栩如生的特质反而增添了一份令人恐惧的微妙理由。

Because we knew nothing about the source of the depiction.

因为我们对这幅画的出处一无所知。

The creature's vast, awesome, and incalculable age was unmistakable.

这只生物体型庞大、令人敬畏、年龄无法估量，这一点毋庸置疑。

But not one link did the depiction show with any known type of art.

但这种描绘方式与任何已知的艺术类型都没有丝毫联系。

Not even the earliest civilizations made reference to this creature.

就连最早的文明都没有提及过这种生物。

But that is not the only point at which our knowledge failed us.

但这并非我们知识失效的唯一原因。

***

The mineralogy of the stone was also a complete mystery.

这种石头的矿物成分也完全是个谜。

Gold specks dotted the soapy, greenish-black stone.

金点缀在皂状的绿黑色石头上。

Iridescent striations ran along the length of the stone.

石头表面沿着长度方向分布着虹彩条纹。

In short, the stone resembled nothing within mineralogy.

简而言之，这块石头在矿物学上与任何石头都截然不同。

Geologists hadn't been able to identify the stone either.

地质学家也一直无法确定这块石头是什么。

The hieroglyphs along the stone were equally baffling.

石头上的象形文字同样令人费解。

The writing system was horribly different than other scripts.

这种文字系统与其他文字截然不同。

A representation of half the world's leading experts was present.

世界一半以上的顶尖专家都出席了会议。

But no link to any known writing system could be established.

但无法确定它与任何已知的文字系统有何关联。

Everything frightfully suggested an old and unhallowed cycle of life.

一切都令人毛骨悚然地暗示着一个古老而邪恶的生命轮回。

A history in which our world and our conceptions played no part.

一段我们的世界和我们的观念都未曾参与的历史。

The experts shook their heads, admitting they had been defeated.

专家们摇了摇头，承认他们失败了。

But one expert did not give up quite so quickly.

但有一位专家并没有这么快放弃。

He claimed to have a touch of bizarre familiarity with the subject.

他声称自己对这个主题有一种奇特的熟悉感。

The monstrous shape and writing weren't entirely new to him.

这种怪异的形状和文字对他来说并非完全陌生。

With some diffidence he told of the odd trifle he knew.

他有些羞怯地讲述了他所知道的一些奇闻轶事。

This person was the late William Channing Webb.

此人是已故的威廉·钱宁·韦伯。

He was professor of anthropology in Princeton University.

他是普林斯顿大学的人类学教授。

And he was an explorer of no small significance.

而且他是一位颇具影响力的探险家。

***

Forty-eight years ago he was exploring Greenland and Iceland.

四十八年前，他曾探索过格陵兰岛和冰岛。

His group were in search of some Runic inscriptions.

他的团队正在寻找一些卢恩文字铭文。

But the expedition failed to unearth any inscriptions.

但探险队未能发现任何铭文。

They trekked the heights of West Greenland's coasts.

他们跋涉攀登了格陵兰岛西部海岸的高地。

Here they encountered a strange cult of degenerate Eskimos.

在这里，他们遇到了一群堕落的爱斯基摩人组成的奇怪邪教。

Their religion consisted of a form of devil-worship.

他们的宗教是一种魔鬼崇拜。

And their rituals were deliberately bloodthirsty and repulsive.

他们的仪式刻意营造出嗜血和令人作呕的氛围。

It was a faith of which other Eskimos knew little.

其他爱斯基摩人对这种信仰知之甚少。

Locals shuddered at the mention of their practices.

当地人一听到他们的习俗就不寒而栗。

They said their believes came from horribly ancient eons.

他们说他们的信仰源自极其古老的时代。

A time before the world as we know it now had ever been made.

在如今我们所知的世界形成之前。

There were human sacrifices and queer hereditary rituals.

那里有活人献祭和怪异的世袭仪式。

And all their worship was directed at a supreme tornasuk.

他们所有的崇拜都指向至高无上的托纳苏克。

Professor Webb had taken a phonetic copy from an aged angekok.

韦伯教授从一本古老的书卷上抄录了一份语音副本。

He had transcribed the wizard-priest's chants as best he could.

他尽其所能地记录下了巫师祭司的咒语。

But currently these transcriptions weren't of prime significance.

但目前这些转录稿并不具有主要意义。

The cult had a cherished stone that they worshipped.

这个邪教组织有一块他们奉为至宝的石头。

They danced wildly when the aurora leaped over the ice cliffs.

当极光跃过冰崖时，他们疯狂地跳舞。

And in the midst of their dance was the strange stone.

在他们翩翩起舞的间隙，出现了一块奇异的石头。

It was, the professor stated, a very crude bas-relief of stone.

教授说，那是一件非常粗糙的石雕浅浮雕。

The stone comprised a hideous picture and some cryptic writing.

石头上刻着一幅可怕的图画和一些晦涩难懂的文字。

And as far as he could tell this stone was a rough parallel.

据他判断，这块石头大致可以与之媲美。

The stone had all the same essential features of bestial things.

这块石头具备所有野兽般事物的基本特征。

The scientists received this data with suspense and astonishment.

科学家们带着紧张和惊讶的心情收到了这些数据。

Even Inspector Legrasse had quickly gained an interest in mythology.

就连勒格拉斯探长也很快对神话产生了兴趣。

And he began at once to ply his informant with questions.

他立刻开始向线人抛出一连串问题。

He had notes of the oral ritual of the cult-worshipers in the swamp.

他有关于沼泽地邪教信徒口头仪式的笔记。

He besought the professor to remember the diabolist Eskimos' chants.

他恳求教授记住爱斯基摩魔鬼的吟唱。

There then followed an exhaustive comparison of details.

随后对细节进行了详尽的比较。

And there then followed a moment of really awed silence.

随后，现场陷入了一阵令人敬畏的沉默。

The Eskimo wizards and the Louisiana swamp-priests were worlds apart.

爱斯基摩巫师和路易斯安那沼泽祭司是截然不同的两个世界。

And yet there was a phrase the two hellish rituals had in common.

然而，这两种地狱般的仪式却有一个共同的短语。

"Ph'nglui mglw'nafh Cthulhu R'lyeh wgah'nagl fhtagn."

"在克苏鲁的莱耶荒冢，他正在沉睡。"

***

Legrasse had one advantage over Professor Webb.

莱格拉斯比韦伯教授有一个优势。

He had spoken to several of his mongrel prisoners.

他曾与几名杂种囚犯交谈过。

Some of them had passed on the phrase's meaning.

他们当中有些人已经将这句话的含义传承了下来。

"In his house at R'lyeh dead Cthulhu waits dreaming."

"死后的克苏鲁在拉莱耶的宅邸中沉睡。"

So the attention turned back to Inspector Legrasse.

于是，大家的注意力又回到了勒格拉斯探长身上。

And he was probed with many disconnected questions.

他被问及许多互不相关的问题。

He detailed his experience with the worshipers from the swamp.

他详细描述了自己与沼泽地信徒们的接触经历。

My uncle attached profound significance to the story.

我的叔叔非常重视这个故事。

The report savored of the wildest dreams of myth-makers.

这份报告充满了造梦者最狂野的幻想。

Theosophists could not have provided more imagination.

即使是神智学家也无法提供如此丰富的想象力。

But the philosophies came from unexpected sources.

但这些理念却来自意想不到的来源。

Half-castes and pariahs told these fantastical stories.

混血儿和贱民讲述了这些奇幻的故事。

On November 1st, 1907, his chain of events unfolded.

1907年11月1日，他的一系列事件展开了。

The New Orleans police received desperate calls.

新奥尔良警方接到了许多绝望的求助电话。

They were called to the swamp and lagoon country to the south.

他们被召集到南部的沼泽和泻湖地区。

The settlers there were mostly primitive, but good-natured.

那里的定居者大多比较原始，但心地善良。

Most living by the swamp were descendants of Lafitte's men.

沼泽地附近的大多数居民都是拉菲特部下的后裔。

But now they were in the grip of stark terror.

但现在他们却陷入了极度的恐惧之中。

An unknown thing had stolen upon them in the night.

夜里，有什么东西悄悄地袭击了他们。

It was voodoo, apparently, that caused the disturbance.

显然，是巫毒术引发了这场骚乱。

But it was a voodoo unlike the other forms of voodoo.

但它与其他形式的巫毒教不同。

Voodoo of a more terrible sort than they had ever known.

一种比他们以往所知的更加可怕的巫毒术。

Some of their women and children had disappeared.

他们的一些妇女和儿童失踪了。

A malevolent drumming had begun its incessant beating.

一阵恶毒的鼓声开始了，持续不断。

Far and deep within those dark, black haunted woods.

在那些阴森黑暗、令人毛骨悚然的森林深处。

There, where no dweller dared to ventured close to.

那里，没有一个居民敢靠近。

There were insane shouts and harrowing screams.

现场充斥着疯狂的叫喊声和令人毛骨悚然的尖叫声。

Soul-chilling chants and dancing devil-flames.

令人毛骨悚然的吟唱和舞动的魔鬼火焰。

The messenger and his people could stand it no more.

信使和他的族人再也无法忍受了。

A body of twenty police set out in the late afternoon.

傍晚时分，二十名警察出发了。

And a shivering settler came with them as a guide.

一位瑟瑟发抖的定居者也随他们一起来了，担任向导。

***

At the end of the passable road they alighted.

他们走到可通行道路的尽头，下了车。

For miles and miles they splashed on in silence.

它们默默地溅起水花，绵延数英里。

And they went on through the terrible cypress woods.

他们继续穿过可怕的柏树林。

Dark, dark woods in which day but almost never came.

幽暗的森林，几乎没有白昼。

Ugly roots set traps for them in the wet ground.

丑陋的根系在潮湿的土壤中设下陷阱，困住它们。

Malignant hanging nooses of Spanish moss beset them.

它们被垂挂的西班牙苔藓绞索所包围。

In the distance the settlement slowly came into sight.

远处，村落渐渐出现在视野中。

Hysterical dwellers ran out of the miserable huts.

惊慌失措的居民们从简陋的小屋里跑了出来。

They clustered around the group of bobbing lanterns.

他们聚集在那群摇曳的灯笼周围。

Far, far ahead the cause of all the fear could be heard.

遥远的前方，传来令人恐惧的根源。

The muffled beat of drums was now faintly audible.

现在隐隐约约能听到沉闷的鼓声。

At times the wind shifted and revealed different sounds.

有时风向改变，带来不同的声音。

Curdling shrieks were audible at infrequent intervals.

不时会听到令人毛骨悚然的尖叫声。

A reddish glare seemed to filter through the undergrowth.

一丝红光似乎透过灌木丛照射进来。

The settlers were reluctant to be left alone again.

定居者们不愿再次被独自留下。

But they point blank refused to move forwards either.

但他们也断然拒绝继续推进。

So the inspector and his colleagues plunged on unguided.

于是，督察和他的同事们便毫无章法地展开了行动。

And they went into the black arcades of horror.

于是，他们走进了恐怖的黑色拱廊。

The region was one of traditionally evil repute.

该地区历来以凶险著称。

The lands were substantially unknown by white men.

白人对这些土地知之甚少。

Not many explorers had traversed those regions yet.

当时很少有探险家涉足那些地区。

There were also legends of a hidden away lake.

还有关于一个隐秘湖泊的传说。

A body of water still unglimpsed by mortal sight.

一片凡人肉眼尚未窥见的水域。

In the lake it was said there dwelt a strange creature.

据说湖里住着一个奇怪的生物。

A huge, formless white polypous thing with luminous eye.

一个巨大的、无定形的白色息肉状物体，长着一只发光的眼睛。

And settlers whispered about bat-winged devils.

定居者们窃窃私语，谈论着长着蝙蝠翅膀的恶魔。

They flew up out of caverns from the inner earth.

它们从地心洞穴中飞了出来。

And together the demons worship it at midnight.

午夜时分，恶魔们会一起膜拜它。

They said it had been there before D'Iberville.

他们说它比迪伊贝尔维尔更早存在。

They said it had been there before La Salle too.

他们说，拉萨尔大学之前那里就有了。

They said it was there before the Native Americans.

他们说它在美洲原住民之前就存在了。

Perhaps it was even there before the wholesome beasts.

或许它甚至比那些温顺的动物还要早存在。

It was a nightmare itself that made men dream.

那本身就是一场噩梦，却也让男人为之着迷。

And to see the thing was the same as death.

亲眼目睹那东西，就如同死亡一般。

And so they had enough warning to know to keep away.

因此，他们有足够的预警时间知道应该远离。

Because it was indeed where they were warned it was.

因为那地方确实如他们之前被警告的那样。

The voodoo orgy was on the fringe of this abhorred area.

这场巫毒狂欢发生在这片令人憎恶的区域边缘。

But the location was already bad enough by itself.

但光是地理位置本身就已经够糟糕的了。

The voodoo activities only added to the horror.

巫毒仪式更增添了恐怖气氛。

Perhaps poetry could do justice to the noises heard.

或许诗歌能够恰当地描绘出所听到的声音。

Otherwise only madness would help one understand.

否则，只有疯狂才能让人理解。

But Legrasse's plowed on through the black morass.

但勒格拉斯已经勇往直前，穿越了这片黑色的泥沼。

The sound of the muffled drumming slowly crystalized.

低沉的鼓声渐渐清晰起来。

And they continued steadily towards the red glare.

他们继续稳步朝着那道红色的光芒走去。

***

There are vocal qualities specific to men.

男性的声音有一些独特的特点。

And there are vocal qualities specific to beasts.

野兽也有其特有的发声特点。

It is terrible when one makes the sounds of the other.

当其中一个发出另一个的声音时，那真是太糟糕了。

Animal fury freed them of their human restraint.

动物的狂暴使他们摆脱了人类的束缚。

Orgiastic license whipped them into demoniac heights.

纵欲的放纵将他们推向了魔鬼般的境地。

Howls that tore through those perpetually dark woods.

撕心裂肺的嚎叫声响彻那片永夜幽暗的森林。

Squawking ecstasies that echoed in everyone's mind.

欢呼雀跃的声音在每个人的脑海中回荡。

Sounds like pestilential tempests from the gulfs of hell.

听起来像是来自地狱深渊的瘟疫风暴。

Now and then the less organized ululations would cease.

偶尔，那些不太有规律的嚎叫声会停止。

A well-drilled chorus of hoarse voices rose in singsong.

一群训练有素、嗓音沙哑的歌者齐声高唱。

And they chanted that hideous phrase of their ritual.

他们齐声吟诵着仪式中那句可怕的咒语。

"Ph'nglui mglw'nafh Cthulhu R'lyeh wgah'nagl fhtagn"

“在克苏鲁的莱耶荒冢，他正在沉睡。”

Then the men reached a spot where the trees were sparser.

然后，他们来到了一处树木较为稀疏的地方。

Suddenly they come in sight of the spectacle itself.

突然间，他们就出现在了壮观景象的视野中。

Four of them reeled from the horrible things they saw.

他们四个人都被眼前的可怕景象吓得魂不附体。

One man fainted, and two were shaken into a frantic cry.

一人昏倒，两人惊恐地发出尖叫。

Fortunately their screams were not heard by other ears.

幸好他们的尖叫声没有被其他人听到。

The mad cacophony of the orgy deadened their screams.

狂欢中疯狂的喧闹声掩盖了他们的尖叫声。

Legrasse splashed swamp water on the fainting man.

勒格拉斯将沼泽水泼向昏厥的男子。

They stood up again, but nearly hypnotized with horror.

他们再次站了起来，但几乎被恐惧催眠了。

In a natural glade of the swamp stood a grassy island.

沼泽地的一片天然空地上，矗立着一座长满青草的小岛。

The grassy island extended perhaps for an acre.

那座长满草的小岛大概绵延一英亩。

And the area was clear of trees and tolerably dry.

而且这片区域没有树木，也比较干燥。

A horde of human abnormality leaped and twisted.

一大群畸形人跳跃扭动。

No Sime could paint what the men were seeing.

任何画家都无法描绘出男人们所看到的景象。

No Angarola has ever painted such an indescribable scene.

安加罗拉从未描绘过如此难以描述的场景。

The hybrid spawn made a monstrous ring-shaped bonfire.

杂交后代燃起了一个巨大的环形篝火。

They brayed bellowed and writhed about in their nudity.

它们赤身裸体地嘶鸣、咆哮、扭动着身体。

Occasionally there were rifts in the curtain of flame.

偶尔，火焰帷幕上会出现裂缝。

And there the object of their worship revealed itself.

在那里，他们崇拜的对象显露出来。

In the midst of the fire stood a great granite monolith.

熊熊烈火之中，耸立着一块巨大的花岗岩巨石。

The stone structure was only about eight feet in height.

这座石砌建筑只有大约八英尺高。

And the noxious carven statuette rested on the monolith.

那尊令人作呕的雕刻小雕像就安放在巨石上。

The idle was almost incongruous in its diminutiveness.

闲散的景象因其渺小而显得格格不入。

Spaced evenly, scaffolds had been erected around the fire.

火堆周围均匀地搭起了脚手架。

From the scaffolding hung a number of marred bodies.

脚手架上悬挂着许多残缺不全的尸体。

The bodies of those that had disappeared from nearby.

附近失踪者的尸体。

It was inside this circle the ring of worshipers were.

信徒们就聚集在这个圆圈之内。

And they roared and jumped in the frantic trance.

他们疯狂地咆哮、跳跃，陷入了恍惚状态。

The general direction of the motion was anti-clockwise.

运动的总体方向是逆时针方向。

The ring of bodies circling around the ring of fire.

一圈圈的尸体围绕着环太平洋火山带旋转。

One man recollected other details even more concerning.

一名男子回忆起其他更令人担忧的细节。

But perhaps the echoes induced him to hear other things.

但或许是回声让他听到了其他声音。

He fancied he heard antiphonal responses to the ritual.

他觉得自己听到了对仪式的回应。

Noises from an unillumined spot deeper within the woods.

从树林深处一个光线昏暗的地方传来声响。

This man, Joseph D. Galvez, I later met and questioned.

后来我遇到了这个人，约瑟夫·D·加尔维斯，并对他进行了讯问。

And he proved to indeed be distractingly imaginative.

事实证明，他确实极富想象力，令人分心。

He even hinted at the faint beating of great wings.

他甚至暗示了巨大翅膀微弱的拍打声。

And he suggested there was a glimpse of shining eyes.

他还暗示，他瞥见了闪亮的眼睛。

And beyond the trees, a mountainous white bulk of something.

树丛之外，耸立着一座白色的山状庞然大物。

I suppose he had heard too much native superstition.

我想他大概是听了太多民间迷信的说法。

But actually the horrified pause was relatively brief.

但实际上，那惊恐的沉默持续时间相对较短。
Duty came first, and they had come to do a job.
职责至上，他们是来工作的。

***

There must have been nearly a hundred mongrel celebrants.
参加庆祝活动的混种动物肯定有近百只。
But the police were able to rely on their firearms.
但警方可以依靠他们的枪支。
And they plunged determinedly into the nauseous rout.
他们毅然决然地踏上了这条令人作呕的征程。
For five minutes the chaotic din was beyond description.
那五分钟的混乱喧嚣简直难以形容。
Wild blows were struck and shots were fired.
双方拳脚相加，枪声四起。
Some escaped arrest by running into the darkness.
有些人逃入夜色中，躲过了逮捕。
They had a better knowledge of the layout of the swamp.
他们对沼泽的地形布局更加了解。
But Legrasse and his men caught around half of them.
但勒格拉斯和他的手下抓住了其中大约一半人。
And they counted around forty-seven sullen prisoners.
他们清点了一下，发现大约有 47 名闷闷不乐的囚犯。
They were forced to put on their clothes again.
他们被迫重新穿上衣服。
And they fell into line between two rows of policemen.
他们排成一列，站在两排警察中间。
Five of the worshipers lay dead by the fire.

五名信徒倒在火海中身亡。

Two severely wounded prisoners were carried away.

两名重伤囚犯被抬走。

Of course the image on the monolith was removed.

当然，巨石上的图像已经被移除了。

Legrasse himself took the evidence to the police station.

勒格拉斯亲自将证据带到了警察局。

The trip back to the headquarters was of intense strain.

返回总部的旅程令人倍感疲惫。

The men were examined when they got back to civilization.

这些人回到文明社会后接受了检查。

The prisoners all proved to be men of a very low type.

这些囚犯个个都是品行低劣的人。

They were all mixed-blooded, and mentally aberrant.

他们都是混血儿，而且精神异常。

Most were seamen by trade, or some similar professions.

他们大多是海员或从事类似职业。

Negroes and mulattoes were sprinkled among them.

其中零星散布着黑人和混血儿。

But most seemed to be West Indians or Brava Portuguese.

但大多数似乎是西印度群岛人或布拉瓦葡萄牙人。

They primarily came from the Cape Verde Islands.

他们主要来自佛得角群岛。

They gave the heterogeneous cult a coloring of voodooism.

他们给这个成分复杂的邪教披上了巫毒教的外衣。

But there wasn't even a need to ask too many questions.

但其实根本没必要问太多问题。

The conclusion quickly became manifest by itself.

结论很快就显而易见了。

Something far deeper than negro fetishism was involved.

这其中牵涉到比黑人恋物癖更深层次的问题。

Although ignorant, but their story was consistent.

虽然他们无知，但他们的说法前后一致。

The creatures all spoke of the same central idea.

这些生物都在谈论同一个中心思想。

They certainly all shared the same loathsome faith.

他们都信奉着同一种令人憎恶的信仰。

They worshiped, so they said, the great old ones.

他们说，他们崇拜的是古老的神灵。

The great old ones lived long before there were any men.

远古邪神生活在人类出现之前很久。

And they came to the young world out of the sky.

它们从天而降，来到了这个年轻的世界。

Those old ones were now gone, they explained.

他们解释说，那些旧的都已经不存在了。

They were now inside the earth and under the sea.

他们现在身处地底，在海底。

But their dead bodies found ways to tell their secrets.

但他们的尸体却以某种方式诉说着他们的秘密。

They whispered into the dreams of the first men.

他们向第一批人类的梦境低语。

And the first men formed a cult which has never died.

而第一批人建立的教派至今从未消亡。

***

The cult had always existed, and always would exist.

这个邪教组织一直存在，而且永远都会存在。

Their followers were hidden in wastes all over the world.

他们的追随者藏身于世界各地的荒漠之中。

Their followers were in dark places explorers overlooked.

他们的追随者身处探险家们忽略的黑暗角落。

And they would remain hidden until they were called.

他们会一直躲藏起来，直到被召唤。

When the great priest Cthulhu rises again to the surface.

当伟大的祭司克苏鲁再次浮出水面时。

When Cthulhu brings the earth again beneath his sway.

当克苏鲁再次将大地置于他的统治之下。

When Cthulhu leaves from his dark house in the mighty city of R'lyeh.

当克苏鲁离开他在雄伟城市拉莱耶的黑暗居所时。

Some day he was going call, when the stars were ready.

总有一天他会召唤，当群星准备就绪之时。

And the secret cult will always be waiting to liberate him.

而那个秘密教派将永远等待着解救他。

Meanwhile, no more of his story must be told.

与此同时，他的故事不能再继续讲下去了。

There was a secret even torture could not extract.

有一个秘密，即使酷刑也无法逼问出来。

Mankind was not alone among the conscious things of earth.

人类并非地球上唯一有意识的生物。

Because shapes came out of the dark to visit the faithful few.

因为黑暗中出现了神秘的身影，前来拜访少数虔诚的信徒。

But these were not the great old ones.

但这并非远古邪神。

No man had ever seen the great old ones.

此前从未有人见过远古邪神。

The carven idol was of great Cthulhu.

那尊雕刻的偶像乃是伟大的克苏鲁。

None could say whether the others were like him.

谁也说不准其他人是否和他一样。

No one could read the old writing now.

现在没人能看懂那些古老的文字了。

Instead, things were told by word of mouth.

相反，事情都是通过口口相传的方式传达的。

The chanted ritual was not the secret.

吟唱的仪式并不是秘密。

The secret was never spoken aloud, only whispered.

这个秘密从未被大声说出口，只是悄悄地流传下来。

The chant meant one thing, and one thing alone:

这句口号只有一个意思，也仅此而已：

"In his house at R'lyeh dead Cthulhu waits dreaming."

"死后的克苏鲁在拉莱耶的宅邸中沉睡。"

Only two of the prisoners were found sane enough to be hanged.

只有两名囚犯被认为神智清醒，可以被处以绞刑。

The rest of them were committed to various institutions.

其余的人都就职于不同的机构。

All denied to have taken any part in the ritual murders.

所有人都否认参与了仪式性谋杀。

They said the killing had been done by something else.

他们说，凶手另有其人。

"The black-winged ones," they each insisted, separately.

"是黑翅膀的那些，"他们各自坚持道。

They had come to them from their immemorial meeting-place.

他们是从他们古老的聚会地点来的。

They had arisen out from the haunted woodlands.

他们从闹鬼的林地中走了出来。

But the stories of mysterious allies were inconsistent.

但关于神秘盟友的说法前后矛盾。

***

What the police did extract came mainly from one man.

警方获取的证据主要来自一名男子。

An immensely aged mestizo named Castro.

一位名叫卡斯特罗的年迈混血儿。

He claimed to have sailed to strange ports.

他声称自己曾航行到过一些陌生的港口。

And he said he had been to the mountains of China.

他说他去过中国的山区。

There he talked with undying leaders of the cult.

在那里，他与该邪教的不死领袖进行了交谈。

Old Castro remembered bits of hideous legend.

老卡斯特罗还记得一些可怕的传说片段。

His legends paled the speculations of theosophists.

他的传奇故事让神智学家们的种种推测黯然失色。

His stories made man seem like a recent creation.

他的故事让人类看起来像是近代才诞生的。

Even the world was transient in his account of things.

在他看来，就连世界也是转瞬即逝的。

There had been eons when other Things ruled on the earth.

在漫长的岁月中，其他事物曾统治着地球。

And they had had great cities here on the earth.

他们在地球上曾拥有过伟大的城市。

The deathless Chinamen told him reserved secrets.

那些不死的中国人告诉他一些秘而不宣的秘密。

He had told him their ruins could still be found.

他曾告诉他，他们的遗迹仍然可以找到。

There were still Cyclopean stones on islands in the Pacific.

太平洋岛屿上仍然散落着巨石。

They all died vast epochs of time before man came.

它们都在人类出现之前的漫长岁月中死去。

But there were knowledges and practices in ancients arts.

但古代艺术中蕴含着知识和实践。

Special rituals which could revive them again, in time.

特殊的仪式或许能让他们死而复生。

In the cycle of eternity their return was inevitable.

在永恒的轮回中，他们的回归是不可避免的。

When the stars come round again to the right positions

当群星再次回到正确的位置时

They had, indeed themselves come from the stars.

它们本身确实来自星辰。

"These great old ones," Castro continued.

"这些伟大的古老者，"卡斯特罗继续说道。

They were not composed entirely of flesh and blood.

它们并非完全由血肉之躯构成。

They had shape," Castro insisted, confidently.

"它们有形状，"卡斯特罗自信地坚持道。

And he had strange proof for what he believed.

而且他还有一套奇怪的证据来证明他所相信的。

But the shape they took on was not made of matter.

但它们呈现出的形状并非由物质构成。

When the stars were in their right positions.

当群星位于正确的位置时。

Then they could plunge from one world to another.

然后他们就可以从一个世界跃入另一个世界。

Because they can move themselves through the sky.

因为它们可以在空中自由移动。

But when the stars were wrong, they cannot live.

但是，当星象出错时，它们就无法生存。

And it is true that they no longer live like we do.

他们的生活方式确实已经和我们不一样了。

But despite that, they never really die either.

但即便如此，他们也从未真正死去。

They rest in stone houses in their great city of R'lyeh.

他们安息在他们伟大的城市拉莱耶的石头房子里。

They are preserved by the spells of mighty Cthulhu.

它们受到强大的克苏鲁的魔法保护。

So there they lie, unaffected by the passing of time.

于是，它们静静地躺在那里，不受时间流逝的影响。

And they wait for another glorious resurrection.

他们等待着另一次荣耀的复活。

When the stars and earth are ready for them again.

当星辰和大地再次准备好迎接它们的时候。

But they are still dependent on an outside force.

但它们仍然依赖于外部力量。

A force from outside served to liberate their bodies.

一股外力解放了他们的身体。

The spells preserved them and kept them intact.

咒语保护了它们，使它们完好无损。

But the spells also kept them from breaking free.

但这些咒语也使他们无法挣脱束缚。

So they could only lie awake in the dark and think.

所以他们只能躺在黑暗中辗转反侧，苦苦思索。

***

In the meantime uncounted millions of years rolled by.

与此同时，无数亿年过去了。

They knew all that was occurring in the universe.

他们了解宇宙中发生的一切。

Because their mode of speech was transmitted thought.

因为他们的说话方式是通过思想传递的。

Even now they were talking in their tombs.

即使到了现在，他们仍在坟墓里交谈。

Then, after infinities of chaos, the first men came.

然后，经过漫长的混沌之后，第一批人类出现了。

The great old ones spoke to the sensitive among them.

古老的神灵们向他们当中那些心思细腻的人诉说着什么。

They spoke to them by molding their dreams.

他们通过塑造人们的梦想与他们交流。

Only that way could their language reach the fleshly minds of mammals.

只有这样，它们的语言才能被哺乳动物的肉体所理解。

Then, whispered Castro, those first men formed the cult.

卡斯特罗低声说道，然后，那些最初的人组成了这个邪教。

They organized themselves around small idols.

他们围绕着一些小偶像组织起来。

The small idols which the great ones had shown them.

那些伟人们向他们展示的小偶像。

Idols brought from dim eras from dark stars.

来自黯淡时代、来自黑暗星辰的偶像。

That cult would never die till the stars came right again.

除非星象再次对调，否则那个邪教永远不会消亡。

The secret priests were going to take great Cthulhu from His tomb.

秘密祭司们打算将伟大的克苏鲁从祂的陵墓中带走。

And they were going to revive His subjects.

他们要复兴祂的子民。

And then Cthulhu was going to resume His rule of earth.

然后克苏鲁将重新统治地球。

The right time was going to reveal itself quite clearly.

合适的时机终会到来。

At that time mankind will have become as the great old ones.

到那时，人类将与远古种族一样伟大。

They will be free and wild and beyond good and evil.

他们将自由自在，无拘无束，超越善恶。

Laws and morals are going to be thrown aside.

法律和道德将被抛诸脑后。

All men will be shouting and killing and reveling in joy.

所有男人都会欢呼、杀戮，并沉浸在欢乐之中。

Then the liberated old ones will teach them the new ways.

然后，那些获得解放的老人们会教他们新的方法。

New ways to shout and kill and revel and enjoy.

呐喊、杀戮、狂欢和享受的新方式。

And all the earth will flame with a holocaust of ecstasy and freedom.

整个地球都将燃起狂喜和自由的烈焰。

Meanwhile the cult had to practice the appropriate rites.

与此同时，该教派必须举行相应的仪式。

They had to keep alive the memory of those ancient ways.

他们必须保留那些古老习俗的记忆。

And they had to shadow forth the prophecy of their return.

他们必须印证他们回归的预言。

In the elder time chosen men spoke with the entombed Old Ones.

在远古时代，被选中的人曾与被埋葬的古神交谈。

The entombed Old Ones spoke to them in their dreams.

被埋葬的古神在他们的梦中与他们交谈。

But then something disturbed their means of communication.

但随后，他们的沟通方式受到了干扰。

The great stone in the city R'lyeh had sunk beneath the waves.

拉莱耶城中的巨石沉入了海底。

And the monoliths and sepulchers were beneath the waters.

而巨石和陵墓则沉没在水下。

Deep waters full of the one primal mystery.

深邃的水域中蕴藏着最原始的奥秘。

Waters through which not even thought can pass.

连思想都无法通过的水。

Water that cut off their spectral communication.

阻断它们光谱通讯的水。

But the memory of the rites and rituals never died.

但这些仪式和习俗的记忆从未消逝。

And high priests said that the city would rise again.

大祭司们说，这座城市将会再次崛起。

When the stars were right Cthulhu was going to return.

当星象预示着克苏鲁即将回归之时。

The moldy black spirits of the earth will come out again.

大地深处那些发霉的黑色精灵还会再次出现。

Shadowy black spirits full of dim rumors.

阴森的黑色幽灵，满腹诡异的谣言。

***

The spirits collected in caverns beneath forgotten sea-bottoms.

聚集在被遗忘的海底洞穴中的灵魂。

But of those spirits old Castro dared not speak much.

但老卡斯特罗不敢多谈那些鬼魂。

And he hurriedly cut himself off from the topic.

他赶紧结束了这个话题。

No amount of persuasion could elicit more in this direction.

无论如何劝说，也无法促使他朝这个方向发展。

No subtlety could convince him to speak of those spirits.

任何委婉的言辞都无法让他谈及那些亡灵。

The size of the old ones, too, he curiously declined to mention.

至于旧物体的尺寸，他却奇怪地拒绝提及。

And of the cult he spoke very little too.

对于这个邪教组织，他也很少提及。

He thought the center lay amid the pathless deserts of Arabia.

他认为中心位于阿拉伯荒凉的沙漠之中。

There in Irem, the City of Pillars, dreams hidden and untouched.

在柱城伊雷姆，隐藏着未曾触及的梦想。

This cult was not allied to the European witch-cult.

这个教派与欧洲的巫术崇拜没有关联。

And the cult was virtually unknown beyond its members.

除了成员之外，这个邪教组织几乎无人知晓。

No book had ever really hinted of their knowledge.

没有任何书籍真正暗示过他们的知识。

Though the deathless Chinamen said the mad Arab Abdul Alhazred came close.

虽然不朽的中国人说，疯狂的阿拉伯人阿卜杜勒·阿尔哈兹雷德曾接近过。

He said that there were double meanings in his Necronomicon.

他说他的《死灵之书》中有双重含义。

The initiated were free to read it if they wanted to.

知情者可以自由阅读。

And they should pay attention to one couplet in particular.

他们尤其应该注意其中的一句诗句。

"That which is not dead can sleep for eternity,"

"凡未死之物，皆可长眠。"

"And with strange eons even death may die."

"在漫长的岁月中，就连死亡也会消亡。"

Legrasse had been deeply impressed by what he heard.

勒格拉斯对所听到的内容印象深刻。

And he was not a little bewildered by the tale.

他听了这个故事后感到十分困惑。

He inquired in vain about the historic affiliations of the cult.

他徒劳地询问了该教派的历史渊源。

Castro, apparently, had told the truth about the oath of secrecy.

显然，卡斯特罗说的关于保密誓言的事是真的。

The authorities at Tulane University could not offer much help either.

杜兰大学的校方也未能提供太多帮助。

The were not able to shed no light upon neither cult, nor the image.

他们既没能揭开邪教的神秘面纱，也没能揭开画像的秘密。

And now the detective had come to the highest authorities in the country.

现在，这位侦探已经把案情报告给了国家最高当局。

And he heard none other than Professor Webb' tale in Greenland.

他在格陵兰岛听到的，正是韦伯教授讲述的故事。

***

Legrasse's tale aroused feverish interest at the meeting.

勒格拉斯的故事在会议上引起了极大的兴趣。

The story was not only significant in its implications.

这个故事的意义不仅在于其蕴含的意义。

But the story was also corroborated by the statuette.

但这座小雕像也证实了这一说法。

The excitement echoed in the subsequent correspondence.

这种兴奋之情在随后的信件往来中再次得到体现。

Those who attended stayed in close contact with each other.

参加者之间保持着密切联系。

Although scant mention occurs in the formal publications.

尽管在正式出版物中鲜有提及。

Caution is the first care of those accustomed to charlatanry.

对于习惯于江湖骗术的人来说，谨慎是首要的。

Impostures are kept out as much as it is possible.

尽可能杜绝冒名顶替行为。

Legrasse for some time lent the image to Professor Webb.

莱格拉斯曾有一段时间将这幅画借给韦伯教授。

But at the latter's death the image was returned to him.

但后者去世后，这幅画像又归还给了他。

And the image remains in Legrasse's possession.

这张照片至今仍由勒格拉斯保存着。

This is where I viewed the terrible image not long ago.

不久前，我就是在这里看到了那张可怕的图片。

The image is unmistakably akin to Wilcox' dream-sculpture.

这幅图像与威尔科克斯的梦幻雕塑有着明显的相似之处。

It was no wonder my uncle was so excited by his tale.

难怪我叔叔对他的故事如此兴奋。

And I'm not surprised he made the efforts he made.

我对他的努力并不感到惊讶。

He had heard everything Legrasse knew of the cult.

他听说了勒格拉斯所知道的关于邪教的一切。

And the strange cultish dreams of a sensitive young man.

以及一位敏感青年的奇怪邪教梦境。

The bas-relief just like the one from the swamp.

这幅浅浮雕和沼泽里的那幅一模一样。

The addition of the devil tablet in Greenland.

格陵兰岛魔鬼石碑的发现。

The exact same words used in three remote occurrences.

在三个互不相干的事件中，使用了完全相同的词语。

The Eskimo diabolists, the mongrels in Louisiana, and then Wilcox.

埃斯基摩恶魔、路易斯安那的杂种，还有威尔科克斯。

What other conclusion could one possibly have come to?

还能得出其他什么结论呢？

It's only natural Professor Angel pursued this conclusion.

安吉尔教授得出这个结论是理所当然的。

And I wouldn't have expected him to be less thorough.

我本不该指望他不够细致。

My great-uncle was a man of principled academic rigor.

我的叔祖父是一位秉持严谨学术原则的人。

Though privately I also had other plausible theories.

虽然私下里我还有其他一些合理的推测。

I suspected young Wilcox of having heard of the cult.

我怀疑年轻的威尔科克斯听说过这个邪教。

Maybe he had heard of the cult in some indirect way.

或许他曾以某种间接的方式听说过这个邪教。

He could easily have invented a series of dreams.

他完全有可能编造了一系列梦境。

That way he could heighten and continue the mystery.

这样他就可以增强并延续这种神秘感。

The dream-narratives and cuttings collected did of course corroborate.

收集到的梦境叙述和剪报当然也印证了这一点。

But the rationalism of my mind had not yet been satisfied.

但我理性的思维还没有得到满足。

Coincidences can form highly believable illusions too.

巧合也能形成高度可信的错觉。

And we have to bear in mind the extravagance of the whole subject.

我们必须牢记整个主题的荒谬之处。

So I was led to adopt what I thought the most sensible conclusions.

因此，我采纳了我认为最明智的结论。

I thoroughly studied the manuscript from the beginning.
我从头到尾仔细研读了这份手稿。
And I correlated the theosophical and anthropological notes.
我将神智学笔记和人类学笔记进行了关联。
I compared the literature with the cult narrative of Legrasse.
我将这部文学作品与勒格拉斯的邪典叙事进行了比较。
I made a trip to Providence to see the sculptor.
我去了一趟普罗维登斯去看那位雕塑家。
And I intended to give him the rebuke I thought proper.
我本打算好好斥责他一番。
There must be consequences, I felt, for the trick he played.
我觉得他耍的这种伎俩必须承担后果。
He had boldly imposed himself upon a learned and aged man.
他竟敢对一位博学多识的老人颐指气使。

***

Wilcox still lived alone where my uncle had met him.
威尔科克斯仍然独自住在我的叔叔遇见他的地方。
In the Fleur-de-Lys Building in Thomas Street.
在托马斯街的百合花大厦。
A hideous Victorian imitation of Seventeenth Century Breton architecture.
维多利亚时代对十七世纪布列塔尼建筑的拙劣模仿。
The building flaunted its stuccoed front amidst its surroundings.
在周围环境中，这座建筑格外引人注目，因为它有着粉刷过的正面。
There were lovely Colonial houses on the ancient hill.

古老的山丘上有一些漂亮的殖民时期房屋。

And the house stood under the shadow of the finest Georgian steeple in America.

而这座房子就矗立在美国最精美的乔治亚式尖顶的阴影之下。

I found him at work in his rooms, among his sculptures.

我发现他正在自己的房间里工作，周围都是他的雕塑作品。

The specimens scattered came from a very unique mind.

散落各处的样本都出自一位非常独特的思想家之手。

At once I conceded that his genius is indeed profound and authentic.

我立刻承认，他的才华的确深邃而真挚。

He has crystallized in clay that which Arthur Machen evokes in prose.

他将亚瑟·梅钦在散文中描绘的事物凝结成了黏土。

He mirrored in marble the nightmares Clark Ashton Smith put to canvas.

他将克拉克·阿什顿·史密斯在画布上描绘的噩梦用大理石重现。

He will, I believe, be spoken of one day as one of the great decadents.

我相信，他终有一天会被人们视为最伟大的颓废派之一。

He was dark, frail, and somewhat unkempt in aspect.

他肤色黝黑，体弱多病，外表有些邋遢。

He turned languidly at my knock on his door.

我敲门时，他懒洋洋地转过身来。

He didn't rise from his seat when I came in.

我进来时，他没有从座位上站起来。

And he asked me what the purpose of my visit was.

他问我此行的目的是什么。

When I told him who I was his interest was piqued.

当我告诉他我是谁时，他来了兴趣。

My uncle had excited his curiosity by probing his strange dreams.

我叔叔探究他那些奇怪的梦境，激起了他的好奇心。

Although he had never explained the reason for the study.

虽然他从未解释过这项研究的原因。

I did not enlarge his knowledge in this regard.

我没有在这方面拓展他的知识。

But I sought with some subtlety to gain his confidence.

但我采取了一些巧妙的手段来赢得他的信任。

In a short time I became convinced of his absolute sincerity.

很快我就确信了他的绝对真诚。

He spoke of the dreams in a manner none could mistake.

他讲述这些梦境的方式，任何人都不会误解。

His dreams' subconscious residuum had influenced his art profoundly.

他的梦境在潜意识中的残留对他的艺术产生了深刻的影响。

He showed me a morbid statue of the likes I had never seen before.

他给我看了一尊我从未见过的令人毛骨悚然的雕像。

The statue's contours almost made me shake with fear.

雕像的轮廓几乎让我吓得浑身发抖。

The potency of the statue's black suggestion was overbearing.

雕像所散发的黑色气息令人难以承受。

He could not recall having seen the original of this thing.

他记不清是否见过这东西的原件。

But the statue was inspired by his own dream bas-relief.

但这座雕像的灵感来源于他自己的梦境浮雕。

The outlines had formed themselves insensibly under his hands.

轮廓在他的手中不知不觉地形成了。

It was, no doubt, the giant shape he had raved of in delirium.

毫无疑问，那就是他在神志不清时胡言乱语的那个巨大形状。

That he really knew nothing of the hidden cult he soon made clear.

他很快就表明，他对这个秘密邪教组织一无所知。

Only my uncle's relentless catechism had given him some clues.

只有我叔叔不厌其烦的教义问答才给了他一些线索。

And again I strove to explain the obvious conclusions away.

于是我又一次试图用各种理由来推翻那些显而易见的结论。

How he could possibly have received the weird impressions?

他怎么可能产生那些奇怪的印象呢？

He talked of his dreams in a strangely poetic fashion.

他用一种奇特的诗意方式谈论他的梦想。

He made me see with terrible vividness the vistas of his dream.

他让我无比清晰地看到了他梦境中的景象。

The damp Cyclopean city of slimy green stone.

潮湿的、由黏糊糊的绿色石头构成的巨石城。

The geometry he oddly said, was all wrong.

他奇怪地说，这个几何图形完全错了。

And he spoke of what he heard with frightened expectancy.

他带着恐惧和期待，讲述着他听到的事情。

The ceaseless, half-mental calling from underground:

地下传来持续不断的、近乎疯狂的呼喊声：

"Cthulhu fhtagn... Cthulhu fhtagn"

"克苏鲁 弗塔格恩… 克苏鲁 弗塔格恩"

These words had formed part of that dreaded ritual.

这些话曾是那令人恐惧的仪式的一部分。

The ritual the told of dead Cthulhu's dream-vigil.

仪式讲述了死去的克苏鲁的梦境守望。

The ritual that told of his stone vault at R'lyeh.

讲述他在拉莱耶的石墓的仪式。

And I felt deeply moved, despite my rational beliefs.

尽管我理性上相信某些事情，但我仍然深受感动。

Wilcox, I was sure, had heard of the cult in some casual way.

我确信威尔科克斯肯定以某种方式听说过这个邪教。

He spent his time in a mass of equally weird literature.

他把时间花在了大量同样怪诞的文学作品中。

He must have forgotten the source of his knowledge.

他一定是忘记了自己知识的来源。

Later the cult had found subconscious expression in his dreams.

后来，这种邪教思想在他的梦境中找到了潜意识的体现。

But this is natural when stories are so impressive.

但当故事如此精彩时，这也很自然。

Finally the cult's ideas manifested themselves in the bas-relief.

最终，该教派的思想体现在了浅浮雕上。

And now the subject of the cult manifested itself in the terrible statue.

现在，邪教的对象显现在了那尊可怕的雕像上。

I was convinced his imposture upon my uncle had been very innocent.

我确信他对我叔叔的欺骗行为完全是无辜的。

He both slightly affected, and slightly ill-mannered.

他既有点矫揉造作，又有点没礼貌。

He had a disposition which I could never like.

他的性格我始终无法喜欢。

But I was willing enough now to admit his genius.

但我现在愿意承认他的才华了。

And I have no way of denying his honesty either.

我也无法否认他的诚实。

Despite my initial feelings, I took leave of him amicably.

尽管我最初有些不快，但我还是友好地和他告别了。

And I wish him all the success his talent promises.

我祝愿他能凭借自己的才华取得应有的成功。

***

The matter of the cult continued to fascinate me.

邪教的事情一直让我很感兴趣。

At times I had visions of the personal fame I could attain.

有时我会幻想自己能获得怎样的个人名望。

I visited New Orleans and talked with Legrasse.

我去了新奥尔良，并与勒格拉斯进行了交谈。

And I spoke with other policemen of that swamp raid.

我还和参与那次沼泽突袭行动的其他警察谈过话。

I saw the frightful image with my own eyes.

我亲眼看到了那可怕的景象。

And I even questioned some of the surviving mongrel prisoners.

我甚至还盘问了一些幸存的杂种囚犯。

Old Castro, unfortunately, had been dead for some years.

不幸的是，老卡斯特罗已经去世多年了。

What I now heard so graphically at first hand excited me afresh.

我亲耳听到的那些生动描述，让我再次兴奋不已。

Though it was really no more than a detailed confirmation.

虽然这实际上只不过是一份详细的确认文件而已。

What they told me I had already read in my uncle's notes.

他们告诉我的内容，我在叔叔的笔记里已经读到过了。

I felt sure that I was on the track of a very real secret.

我确信自己正在追踪一个非常真实的秘密。

And I was sure I was going to discover a very ancient religion.

我当时确信自己会发现一种非常古老的宗教。

The discovery would make me an anthropologist of note.

这一发现将使我成为一位知名的民族学家。

My attitude was still one of absolute rational materialism.

我的态度仍然是绝对理性唯物主义。

And I wish my attitude to the subject matter had not changed.

我希望我对这个话题的态度没有改变。

I discounted with almost inexplicable perversity the coincidences.

我近乎疯狂地忽略了这些巧合。

The dream notes and odd cuttings collected by Professor Angell.

安吉尔教授收集的梦境笔记和零散剪报。

One thing I began to doubt was the cause of my uncle's death.

我开始怀疑的一件事是叔叔的死因。

I began to suspect his death was far from natural.

我开始怀疑他的死并非自然死亡。

And I now fear I know my uncle's death was not natural.

我现在担心我知道我叔叔的死并非自然死亡。

It was on a narrow hill street where he fell.

他是在一条狭窄的山路上摔倒的。

The street lead up from the ancient waterfront.

这条街道从古老的海滨向上延伸。

The port-town swarms with foreign mongrels.

这座港口城市里到处都是外国杂种狗。

He fell after a careless push from a negro sailor.

他被一名黑人水手不小心推了一下就摔倒了。

I had not forgotten the mixed blood of the cult-members in Louisiana.

我没有忘记路易斯安那州邪教成员的混血血统。

I had not forgotten the sailors in the voodoo orgy.

我没有忘记那些参加巫毒狂欢的水手们。

And would not be surprised to learn that they had other knowledge too.

如果得知他们还掌握其他知识，我也不会感到惊讶。

Secret methods as anciently known as the cryptic rites.

古代被称为神秘仪式的秘密方法。

Poison needles as ruthless their demonic beliefs.

毒针象征着他们恶魔般的信仰，冷酷无情。

Legrasse and his men, it is true, have been let alone.

的确，勒格拉斯和他的部下被放过了。

But in Norway a certain seaman who saw things is dead.

但在挪威，一位目睹过某些事情的水手已经去世了。

Might not sinister ears have picked up my uncle's interest in the sculptor?

会不会是心怀不轨的人察觉到了我叔叔对那位雕塑家的兴趣？

Might not the deeper inquiries of my uncle have drawn someone's attention?

我叔叔更深入的询问会不会引起某些人的注意？

I think Professor Angell died because he knew too much.

我认为安吉尔教授的死是因为他知道得太多了。

Or he died because he was likely to learn too much.

或者他死是因为他可能学到了太多东西。

Whether I shall go out as he did remains to be seen.

我是否会像他那样出去，还有待观察。

Because I too have learned much about Cthulhu.

因为我也对克苏鲁了解了很多。

The Madness from the Sea
来自海洋的疯狂

There is one great boon heaven could grant me.

上天可以赐予我一件莫大的恩惠。

The total effacing of the results of a mere chance.

完全抹杀偶然事件的结果。

I wish I had never seen that stray piece of paper.

我真希望从未见过那张散落的纸片。

My daily routine would normally not have taken me there.

我的日常作息通常不会带我去那里。

On any other day I would not have noticed anything.

换作平时，我根本不会注意到任何异常。

It was an old number of an Australian journal.

这是澳大利亚一份期刊的旧刊号。

The Sydney Bulletin for April 18, 1925

1925年4月18日悉尼公报

The paper had even slipped past the cutting bureau.

这份文件甚至连截稿处都没过。

I had largely given over my inquiries to a friend.

我基本上把调查工作委托给了朋友。

He had taken on the work of most of the research.

他承担了大部分研究工作。

He had come to refer to the group as the "Cthulhu Cult".

他后来把这个组织称为“克苏鲁教”。

I was visiting my learned friend of Paterson, New Jersey.

我当时正在拜访我住在新泽西州帕特森市的一位博学的朋友。

The curator of a local museum, and a mineralogist of note.

当地博物馆馆长，同时也是一位知名的矿物学家。

While at his museum I had access to the reserved specimens.

在他的博物馆里，我有机会接触到馆藏的标本。

And this is when an odd picture caught my attention.

这时，一张奇怪的照片引起了我的注意。

Beneath one of the stones was the Sydney Bulletin I mentioned.

其中一块石头下面是我提到的那份《悉尼公报》。

My friend has wide affiliations in all conceivable foreign lands.

我的朋友在所有你能想象到的外国都有广泛的人脉关系。

The picture was a half-tone cut of a hideous stone image.

图片是一张丑陋的石头图像的半色调切割图。

Almost identical with the stone Legrasse had found in the swamp.

几乎与勒格拉斯在沼泽中发现的石头一模一样。

Eagerly I read the article for its precious contents.

我迫不及待地阅读了这篇文章，因为它内容宝贵。

But I was disappointed to find that it was just a short article.

但令我失望的是，它只是一篇短文。

Although brief, the information was of portentous significance.

虽然篇幅简短，但信息意义重大。

"MYSTERY DERELICT FOUND AT SEA"
"海上发现神秘废弃船只"

Vigilant Arrives With Helpless Armed New Zealand Yacht in Tow.

警惕号拖着毫无防备的武装新西兰游艇抵达。

One Survivor and one Dead Man Found Aboard.

船上发现一名幸存者和一名死者。

Tale of Desperate Battle and Deaths at Sea.

一场殊死搏斗和海上死亡的故事。

Rescued Seaman Refuses Particulars of Strange Experience.

获救海员拒绝透露其奇怪经历的细节。

Odd Idol Found in His Possession, Inquiry to Follow.

在其身上发现一件奇特偶像，将展开调查。

The Alert of Dunedin yacht, N.Z., had been disabled in battle.

新西兰达尼丁的"警戒号"游艇在战斗中被击毁。

Previously the ship had left from Valparaiso on March 25th.

此前，该船于3月25日从瓦尔帕莱索出发。

On April 2nd the ship was driven considerably south of her course.

4月2日，这艘船偏离航线向南行驶了相当远的距离。

Exceptionally heavy storms had redirected the ship.

异常猛烈的风暴改变了船只的航向。

Monster waves forced the ship to take a different route.

巨浪迫使船只改道航行。

On April 12th the ship was sighted by another ship.

4月12日，另一艘船发现了这艘船。

Latitude 34° 21', Longitude 152° 17'

纬度 34° 21'，经度 152° 17'

Initially they thought the ship had been deserted.

起初他们以为船上无人居住。

But one still living man had been found on board.

但船上还发现了一名活着的男子。

This lone survivor was in a half-delirious condition.

这名唯一的幸存者当时处于半谵妄状态。

The only other victim found was a man already dead a week.

发现的另一名受害者是一名一周前已经死亡的男子。

Now the heavily armed steam yacht was being towed.

现在，这艘装备精良的蒸汽游艇正被拖走。

And this morning the ship was coming in to its wharf.

今天早上，这艘船正驶入码头。

The living man was clutching a horrible stone idol.

那个活着的人手里紧紧抱着一个可怕的石像。

The stone idol was about a foot in height.

这尊石像大约一英尺高。

And the origins of the stone were completely unknown.

而这块石头的来历则完全是个谜。

Authorities at Sydney university were baffled.

悉尼大学的校方对此感到困惑不解。

The Royal Society couldn't offer information about the idol.

英国皇家学会无法提供有关该偶像的信息。

And the Museum in College street had no insights either.

学院街上的博物馆也毫无启发。

The survivor says he found the stone in the cabin of the yacht.

幸存者称，他在游艇船舱里发现了这块石头。

Allegedly the idol was in a small carved shrine.

据说，这尊神像被放置在一个小型雕刻神龛中。

And the carvings of the shrine were of common pattern.

神龛上的雕刻图案都很常见。

This man eventually recovered back to his senses.

这个人最终恢复了神智。

And he told an exceedingly strange story of piracy and slaughter.

他讲述了一个极其离奇的海盗和屠杀故事。

He is Gustaf Johansen, a Norwegian of some intelligence.

他名叫古斯塔夫·约翰森，是一位颇具才智的挪威人。

And he had been second mate of the two-masted schooner Emma of Auckland.

他曾是奥克兰双桅帆船"艾玛号"的二副。

The ship sailed for Callao February 20th, manned by eleven sailors.

2月20日，该船启程前往卡亚俄，船上有11名水手。

The ship, he says, was delayed and thrown widely south of her course.

他说，这艘船延误了，并且偏离航线向南行驶了很远。

There was a great storm on March 1st, and on March 22nd.

3月1日和3月22日都发生了大风暴。

On their journey they encountered another ship.

旅途中，他们遇到了另一艘船。

This was in S. Latitude 49° 51′, W. Longitude 128° 34′

这里位于南纬49°51′，西经128°34′。

This ship was manned by a queer and evil-looking crew.

这艘船上的船员长相怪异邪恶。

All the men were of Kanakas and half-castes.

所有男子都是卡纳卡人和混血儿。

Being ordered peremptorily to turn back, Capt. Collins refused.

科林斯上尉被命令立即返回，但他拒绝了。

Without warning the strange crew began to shoot savagely upon the schooner.

毫无预警，这群奇怪的船员开始向帆船疯狂射击。

They shot a peculiarly heavy battery of brass cannon.

他们发射了一门异常沉重的黄铜炮。

The men from his ship showed fighting spirit, says the survivor.

幸存者说，他船上的水手们展现出了顽强的斗志。

The schooner began to sink from shots beneath the waterline.

由于水下中弹，帆船开始下沉。

But they managed to heave alongside their enemy boat, and board her.

但他们设法靠近了敌舰，并登上了敌舰。

They grappled with the savage crew on the yacht's deck.

他们与游艇甲板上的凶残船员展开了搏斗。

Their mode of fighting seemed to be strangely clumsy.

他们的战斗方式显得异常笨拙。

But defeat did not seem to be an option for these savage men.

但对于这些野蛮人来说，失败似乎不是一种选择。

They had a particularly abhorrent and desperate way of fighting.

他们的战斗方式极其残忍和绝望。

So they had no choice but to kill all men of the enemy ship.

所以他们别无选择，只能杀死敌船上的所有人员。

Three of their men were also killed in the fight.

他们的三名手下也在战斗中丧生。

Capt. Collins and First Mate Green were among the dead.

科林斯船长和格林大副也在遇难者之列。

Second Mate Johansen took over control from First Mate Green.

二副约翰森从大副格林手中接管了指挥权。

And the remaining eight men proceeded to navigate the captured yacht.

剩下的八个人则继续驾驶着缴获的游艇。

They proceeded to continue in the original direction they were going.

他们继续朝着原来的方向前进。

To see if there had been any reason they were ordered to turn around.

为了查明他们是否有什么理由被命令掉头。

***

The next day, it appears, they landed on a small island.

第二天，他们似乎在一个小岛上登陆了。

Although no island is known to exist in that part of the ocean.

虽然目前尚未发现该海域存在任何岛屿。

Six of the men somehow died ashore while on the island.

岛上有六名男子不知何故在岸上丧生。

Though Johansen is queerly reticent about this part of his story.

不过，约翰森对故事的这一部分却出奇地不愿多谈。

And he speaks only of their falling into a rock chasm.

他只提到他们掉进了岩石深渊。

Later, it seems, he and one companion boarded the yacht.

后来，他似乎和一位同伴登上了游艇。

Together they tried to sail the ship, undermanned.

他们人手不足，却一起尝试驾驶这艘船。

But they were beaten about by the storm of April 2nd.

但他们却在4月2日的暴风雨中遭受了重创。

From that time till his rescue on the 12th, the man remembers little.

从那时到12日获救，这名男子几乎什么都不记得了。

And he does not even recall when William Briden, his companion, died.

他甚至不记得他的同伴威廉·布里登是什么时候去世的。

Autopsy could reveal no obvious cause to Briden's death.

尸检未能发现布里登的明显死因。

The most likely cause of death is exposure to the elements.

最可能的死因是暴露于恶劣天气环境中。

The Dunedin reported that their boat, the Alert, was well known.

达尼丁人报告说，他们的船"警戒号"很有名。

The island traders bore an evil reputation along the waterfront.

岛上的商人在沿海地区名声很差。

The ship was owned by a curious group of half-castes.

这艘船的主人是一群古怪的混血儿。

Frequent meetings and night trips to the woods attracted curiosity.

频繁的聚会和夜间去树林的旅行引起了人们的好奇。

The ship had set sail in great haste on March 1st.

3月1日，这艘船匆匆启航。

Just after the storm, and the earth tremors that night.

暴风雨过后，当晚大地颤抖。

Our Auckland correspondent gives the Emma excellent reputation.

我们的奥克兰通讯员给予艾玛极佳的评价。

The Crew from the Emma were held very in high regard.

"艾玛"号上的船员们备受尊敬。

And Johansen is described as a sober and worthy man.

约翰森被描述为一个稳重而值得尊敬的人。

The admiralty will institute an inquiry on the whole matter.

海军部将对整件事展开调查。

Starting tomorrow they will collect all relevant information.

从明天开始，他们将收集所有相关信息。

Every effort will be made to induce Johansen to speak.

我们将尽一切努力促使约翰森开口说话。

This and the hellish image were all the information I had to go on.

这些信息和那张可怕的图片就是我掌握的全部线索。

But what a train of ideas that little information started in my mind!

但这点信息却在我脑海中引发了一连串的想法！

Here were new treasuries of data on the Cthulhu Cult.

这里保存着关于克苏鲁教的新资料宝库。

The cult not only had interests on land.

这个邪教组织不仅在土地上有利益。

Now there was evidence they also had connections to the sea.

现在有证据表明，他们也与海洋有联系。

What motive prompted the hybrid crew to order back the Emma?

是什么动机促使混血船员们下令召回艾玛号？

Why did they sail about with their hideous idol?

他们为何带着那丑陋的偶像四处航行？

What was the unknown island on which six of the Emma's crew had died?

艾玛号上的六名船员丧生的那个未知岛屿是哪里？

And why was Johansen so secretive about their death?

为什么约翰森对他们的死讯讳莫如深？

What had the vice-admiralty's investigation brought out?

海军中部的调查结果是什么？

And what was known of the noxious cult in Dunedin?

人们对达尼丁的那个邪恶邪教了解多少？

Nor could one help but marvel at the timing of the events.

人们不禁对这些事件发生的时机感到惊讶。

There was a deep and more than natural linkage between the dates.

这些日期之间存在着深刻而又非同寻常的联系。

A malign and now undeniable significance to the various turns of events.

对事态的各种发展具有恶劣且如今不可否认的意义。

***

My uncle had noted with great care the connecting events.

我叔叔非常仔细地记录了所有相关事件。

On March 1st the earthquake and storm had come.

3月1日，地震和风暴来临。

February 28th, according to the International Date Line.

根据国际日期变更线，日期为2月28日。

From Dunedin the noisome crew of the Alert darted eagerly forth.

从达尼丁出发的"警戒号"上，那群吵闹的船员急切地向前冲去。

They moved as if they had been imperiously summoned.

他们行动起来，仿佛是被专横召见一般。

On the other side of the earth the other events unfolded.

在地球的另一端，其他事件也随之发生。

Poets and artists had begun to have their strange dreams.

诗人艺术家们开始做一些奇怪的梦。

Dreams of a dank Cyclopean city from times long gone.

梦见一座来自远古时代的阴暗潮湿的独眼巨人之城。

A young sculptor was persuaded by these dreams too.

一位年轻的雕塑家也被这些梦境所打动。

In his sleep he molded the form of the dreaded Cthulhu.

他在睡梦中塑造了可怕的克苏鲁的形象。

On March 23rd the crew of the Emma landed on an unknown island.

3月23日，"艾玛"号的船员们登陆了一座不知名的岛屿。

There on that island they left six men dead.

他们在那个岛上留下了六具尸体。

On that date the dreams of sensitive men assumed a heightened vividness.

在那一天，敏感男人的梦境变得格外生动。

Their dreams darkened with dread of a giant monster's malign pursuit.

他们的梦境因对巨型怪物恶意追捕的恐惧而变得阴暗。

One architect went mad from his dreams that night.

那晚，一位建筑师因噩梦而发疯。

And a sculptor had lapsed suddenly into delirium!

一位雕塑家突然陷入了谵妄状态！

And then there was the storm of April 2nd.

然后，4月2日又发生了那场暴风雨。

The date on which all dreams of the dank city ceased.

关于那座阴暗城市的梦想彻底破灭的那一天。

Wilcox emerged unharmed from the bondage of strange fever.

威尔科克斯毫发无损地从这种怪病的折磨中解脱出来。

And everything appeared to be normal again.

一切似乎又恢复了正常。

But what about the hints old Castro had suggested?

但是老卡斯特罗曾暗示过的那些话又该怎么解释呢？

What about the sunken, star-born old ones?

那么那些沉没的、诞生于星辰的古老种族呢？

What about their promised return and coming reign?

他们承诺的回归和即将到来的统治呢？

What about their faithful cult and their mastery of dreams?

那么，他们忠实的信徒和他们对梦境的掌控又该如何解释呢？

Was I tottering on the brink of cosmic horrors?

我当时是否正徘徊在宇宙恐怖的边缘？

Cosmic horrors far beyond man's power to bear?

远超人类承受能力的宇宙恐怖？

If so, they must be horrors of the mind alone.

如果真是如此，那它们一定只是人们想象中的恐怖。

On the second of April there was sudden coordinated calm.

4月2日，突然出现了协调一致的平静。

The monstrous menace that sieged mankind's soul had vanished.

曾经笼罩人类灵魂的巨大威胁已经消失了。

That evening I made all necessary arrangements for onwards travel.

当晚我为接下来的行程做好了所有必要的安排。

I bade my host adieu and took a train for San Francisco.

我向房东告别，乘火车前往旧金山。

***

In less than a month I was at the port of Dunedin.

不到一个月，我就抵达了达尼丁港。

Here, however, my investigation stumbled slightly.

然而，我的调查在这里遇到了一些小麻烦。

I inquired in the old sea taverns where the men had lingered.

我打听了一下那些男人曾经逗留过的老式海边酒馆。

But little was known of the strange cult members.

但人们对这个神秘邪教的成员知之甚少。

Waterfront scum was far too common for special mention.

码头区的渣滓实在太常见了，无需特别提及。

But there was vague talk about one inland trip these mongrels had made.

但有人含糊地提到，这些杂种狗曾进行过一次内陆旅行。

Faint drumming and red flames were noted on the distant hills.

远处山丘上隐隐传来鼓声和红色火焰。

In Auckland I learned only a little more of Johansen.

在奥克兰，我对约翰森的了解又少了一些。

He had been taken to Sydney for the investigation.

他已被带到悉尼接受调查。

A perfunctory and inconclusive questioning turned his hair white.

敷衍了事、毫无结果的询问让他白了头发。

Thereafter he sold his cottage in West Street.

之后他卖掉了位于西街的小屋。

And he sailed with his wife to his old home in Oslo.

然后他和妻子乘船回到了他在奥斯陆的老家。

His experience had clearly stirred him deeply.

他的经历显然深深触动了他。

But he told his friends no more than he had told the admiralty officials.

但他告诉朋友的，和告诉海军部官员的一样多。

And all they could do was to give me his Oslo address.

他们所能做的，只是给了我他的奥斯陆地址。

After that I went to Sydney and talked profitlessly with seamen.

之后我去了悉尼，和海员们进行了毫无收获的交谈。

Members of the vice-admiralty court could not enlighten me either.

海军副法庭的成员们也无法给我解答。

I tracked the Alert down to Circular Quay in Sydney Cove.

我追踪到警报地点位于悉尼湾的环形码头。

The ship had been sold and was again in commercial use.

这艘船已被出售，并重新投入商业运营。

But I could gain no further clues from the ship's cargo.

但我无法从船上的货物中获得任何进一步的线索。

The image was preserved in the Museum at Hyde Park.

这张照片被保存在海德公园博物馆。

The cuttlefish head, dragon body, and scaly wings.

乌贼头、龙身、鳞片翅膀。

The monster crouching atop the hieroglyphed pedestal.

怪物蹲伏在刻有象形文字的基座上。

I studied every detail of the idol long and well.

我仔细研究了偶像的每一个细节。

The relic was a thing of balefully exquisite workmanship.

这件圣物做工精美绝伦，却也透着一丝不祥之兆。

I couldn't help but notice the similarity to Legrasse's smaller specimen.

我不禁注意到它与勒格拉斯较小的标本很相似。

Both idols had the same utter mystery and terrible antiquity.

这两个偶像都充满了神秘感和令人敬畏的古老气息。

And both idols had the same unearthly strangeness of material.

这两个偶像都具有同样超凡脱俗的材质特征。

Geologists, the curator told me, had found it a monstrous puzzle.

馆长告诉我，地质学家们发现这是一个巨大的谜题。

They insisted that the world held no rock like this one.

他们坚称世界上没有像这样的岩石。

Then I thought with a shudder of what old Castro had told Legrasse.

然后，我打了个寒颤，想起了老卡斯特罗告诉勒格拉斯的话。

The tale of the primal great ones, sunken under the sea.

讲述的是沉没于海底的远古伟大存在的故事。

"They had come from the stars."

"他们来自星空。"

"They had brought their images with them."

"他们把自己的画像也带来了。"

I was shaken with a mental revolution as I had never before known.

我经历了一场前所未有的精神革命。

I was now completely resolved to visit Mate Johansen in Oslo.

我下定决心要去奥斯陆拜访马特·约翰森。

Sailing for London, I re-embarked at once for the Norwegian capital.

我乘船前往伦敦，随即又换乘前往挪威首都的船只。

And one autumn day I landed at the wharves.

秋日的一天，我来到了码头。

***

Johansen's hometown was in the shadow of the Egeberg.

约翰森的家乡位于埃格贝格山脚下。

I discovered he lived in the Old Town of King Harold Haardrada.

我发现他住在哈罗德国王哈德拉达老城。

For centuries the greater city had masqueraded as "Christiania".

几个世纪以来，这座大城市一直伪装成"克里斯蒂安尼亚"。

King Harald Hardrada kept alive the name of Oslo.

哈拉尔·哈德拉达国王保留了奥斯陆的名字。

I made the brief trip to his residences by taxicab.

我乘出租车很快就到了他的住处。

A neat and ancient building with plastered front.

一栋整洁古老的建筑，正面抹了灰泥。

And I knocked with palpitant heart at the door.

我心跳加速，敲响了房门。

A sad-faced woman in black answered my summons.

一位面容悲伤、身穿黑衣的女子应召而来。

I was stung with disappointment at the sight.

看到这一幕，我感到无比失望。

She told me in halting English that Gustaf Johansen was no more.

她用不太流利的英语告诉我，古斯塔夫·约翰森已经去世了。

He had not long survived his return, said his wife.

他的妻子说，他回来后没过多久就去世了。

The doings at sea in 1925 had broken him.

1925 年海上遭遇的经历彻底击垮了他。

He had told her no more than he had told the public.

他告诉她的和告诉公众的并无二致。

But he had left a long manuscript of "technical matters".

但他留下了一份篇幅很长的"技术性文件"。

These notes of the voyage had been written in English.

这些航行笔记是用英文写的。

Evidently in order to safeguard her from the peril of casual perusal.

显然是为了保护她免受随意翻阅的危险。

He had gone for a walk through a narrow lane near the Gothenburg dock.

他沿着哥德堡码头附近的一条狭窄小巷散步。

A bundle of papers falling from an attic window had knocked him down.

从阁楼窗户掉下来的一捆文件把他砸倒了。

Two Lascar sailors at once helped him to his feet.

两名拉斯卡尔水手同时把他扶了起来。

But before the ambulance could reach him he was dead.

但救护车赶到之前，他已经去世了。

The physicians found no adequate cause for his death.

医生们没有找到他死亡的充分原因。

They mostly attributed his death to heart trouble.

他们大多将他的死因归咎于心脏病。

But they added his weakened constitution most likely contributed.

但他们补充说，他体质虚弱很可能也是原因之一。

I now felt a deep gnawing at my vitals.

我感到体内深处仿佛被狠狠地啃噬着。

A dark terror which will never leave me till I, too, am at rest.

一种挥之不去的黑暗恐惧，直到我也获得安息，它才会离开我。

Whether my death will come "accidentally" or not I can't tell.

我无法预知我的死亡是"意外"还是"有意"。

I spoke to the widow about her husband's work.

我和这位寡妇谈了谈她丈夫的工作。

And I persuaded her I had a "technical" connection to him.

我成功说服了她，我与他有"技术"上的联系。

So she felt I was sufficiently entitled to the manuscript.

所以她觉得我有充分的权利获得这份手稿。

And so I attained the dead man's writing.

于是，我得到了死者的遗稿。

I began to read the documents on the boat to London.

我在前往伦敦的船上开始阅读这些文件。

They were little more than simple, rambling notes.

它们只不过是一些简单、杂乱的笔记而已。

A naive sailor's effort at a post-facto diary.

一位天真的水手事后尝试写的日记。

He strove to recall that last awful voyage day by day.

他努力日复一日地回忆起那次可怕的航行。

I cannot attempt to transcribe his notes verbatim.

我无法逐字逐句地转录他的笔记。

The manuscript is clouded with vagueness and redundance.

这份手稿含糊不清，内容冗余。

But I will tell the gist of what he wrote.

但我会概括他所写的内容。

Perhaps then you will understand why I stuffed my ears with cotton.

或许那样你就能明白我为什么用棉花塞住耳朵了。

The sound of the water against the vessel's sides became unendurable.

水拍打船舷的声音变得令人难以忍受。

***

Johansen, thank God, did not quite know what he had seen.

谢天谢地，约翰森并不完全清楚他看到了什么。

But it is evident he had seen the city and the Thing.

但很明显，他已经见过那座城市和那个东西。

I shall never sleep calmly again when I think of the horrors.

每当想起那些恐怖的景象，我再也无法安然入睡。

The horrors that lurk ceaselessly behind life in time and space.

在时间和空间中，生命背后始终潜伏着的恐怖。

Those unhallowed blasphemies that come from elder stars.

那些来自远古星辰的亵渎神明的话语。

Dreamers beneath the sea known only by a nightmare cult.

海底的梦魇，只有噩梦教派才知道他们的存在。

A cult ready and eager to release these monsters into the world.

一个邪教组织已经准备好并渴望将这些怪物释放到世上。

Whenever another earthquake raises their monstrous stone city again.

每当另一场地震再次将他们那座巨大的石头城市隆起。

When Cthulhu is under the light of the sun once more.

当克苏鲁再次沐浴在阳光下。

Johansen's voyage had begun just as he told it to the vice-admiralty.

约翰森的航行正如他向海军部副部长所描述的那样开始了。

The Emma, in ballast, had cleared Auckland on February 20th.

2月20日，空载的"艾玛"号驶离奥克兰。

The ship had felt the full force of that earthquake-born tempest.

这艘船充分感受到了那场地震引发的风暴的威力。

The horrors from the sea-bottom that filled men's dreams.

那些充斥着男人噩梦的海底恐怖景象。

Once under control again the ship was making good progress.

一旦重新控制住船只，它就进展顺利。

But then the ship was held up by the Alert on March 22nd.

但随后，这艘船在 3 月 22 日被"警戒"号拦下。

I could feel the mate's regret as he wrote of her bombardment and sinking.

从他描述她被炮火轰击和沉没时的懊悔之情中，我能感受到这位船员的遗憾。

Of the swarthy cult-fiends on the other boat he speaks with horror.

他惊恐地谈起另一艘船上那些皮肤黝黑的邪教恶魔。

There was some peculiarly abominable quality about them.

他们身上有一种极其令人厌恶的特质。

Something made their destruction seem almost a duty.

某种东西让毁灭他们似乎成了一种责任。

This point was brought up during the proceedings of the court of inquiry.

这一点在调查法庭的审理过程中被提出。

Johansen shows ingenuous wonder at the accusation of ruthlessness.

约翰森对被指控冷酷无情表示出天真的惊讶。

Curiosity is what drove the men on in their captured yacht.

好奇心驱使着这些人驾驶着被俘获的游艇继续前进。

Sticking out of the sea the men sighted a great stone pillar.

男人们发现海面上耸立着一根巨大的石柱。

In South Latitude 47° 9', West Longitude 126° 43' they come upon a coastline.

在南纬 47° 9'，西经 126° 43'，他们来到了海岸线。

The coastline was of mingled mud, ooze, and weedy Cyclopean masonry.

海岸线由泥浆、淤泥和长满杂草的巨型石块混合而成。

Nothing less than the tangible substance of earth's supreme terror.

这就是地球上最恐怖事物的有形体现。

They had come across the nightmare corpse-city of R'lyeh.

他们发现了噩梦般的尸体之城拉莱耶。

A city built in measureless eons behind history.

一座历经漫长岁月才建成的城市。

Monuments to vast loathsome shapes that seeped down from the dark stars.

那是巨大而令人厌恶的形状的纪念碑，它们从黑暗的星辰中渗出。

There lay great Cthulhu and his hordes for incalculable cycles.

伟大的克苏鲁和他的大军在那里沉睡了无数个轮回。

Hidden in green slimy vaults, they sent out their thoughts.

他们躲在绿色黏糊糊的密室里，发出自己的思想。

The thoughts that spread fear to the dreams of the sensitive.

那些在敏感者的梦境中散播恐惧的想法。

The thoughts that called imperiously to the faithful.

那些威严地召唤信徒的思想。

"Come on a pilgrimage of liberation and restoration."

"来吧，踏上解放与复兴的朝圣之旅。"

All this horror Johansen had no way of suspecting.

约翰森对这一切恐怖事件都毫不知情。

But God knows he had soon seen enough!

但上帝知道，他很快就看够了！

I suppose what they saw was only a single mountain-top.

我想他们看到的只是一座山顶。

Soon the rest of the city emerged from the waters.

不久，城市的其余部分也从水中浮现出来。

The hideous monolith-crowned citadel where great Cthulhu was buried.

克苏鲁神被埋葬的，是那座耸立着可怕巨石的堡垒。

I shudder to think of all that may be brooding down there.

一想到下面可能潜伏着什么，我就不寒而栗。

And I almost wish to kill myself to stop these thoughts.

我几乎想自杀来阻止这些想法。

***

Johansen and his men were awed by the cosmic majesty.

约翰森和他的部下被宇宙的壮丽景象所震撼。

They beheld the sight of this dripping Babylon of elder demons.

他们目睹了这座由远古恶魔建造的、滴着水的巴比伦城的景象。

They must have guessed without guidance what it was they saw.

他们一定是在没有指导的情况下猜到了自己所看到的是什么。

What they saw was nothing of this or of any sane planet.

他们所看到的，既不属于这个星球，也不属于任何一个正常的星球。

The unbelievable size of the greenish stone blocks.

这些绿色的石块体积之大令人难以置信。

The dizzying height of the great carven monolith.

巨大的雕刻巨石令人眩晕的高度。

And then there was the bas-reliefs found on the captured ship.

此外，在缴获的船只上还发现了浅浮雕。

The colossal statues mirrored the scene on the carvings.

这些巨大的雕像与雕刻上的场景遥相呼应。

Johansen achieved something very close to futurism.

约翰森的作品非常接近未来主义。

Because he did not describe any definite structure or building.

因为他没有描述任何具体的结构或建筑物。

He dwelled on the broad impressions of vast angles and stone surfaces.

他沉浸于广阔的棱角和石质表面的深刻印象中。

Surfaces too great to belong to anything right or proper for this earth.

面积太大，不属于地球上任何合适的或恰当的范畴。

Surfaces impious with horrible images and hieroglyphs.

表面污秽不堪，布满可怕的图像和象形文字。

There is a reason I mention his talk about angles.

我之所以提到他关于角度的演讲，是有原因的。

It reminds me of something Wilcox had told me of his awful dreams.

这让我想起威尔科克斯跟我讲过的他做的可怕梦。

He had said that the geometry of the dream-place he saw was abnormal.

他曾说过，他梦中所见之地的几何形状是不正常的。

Non-Euclidean spheres unlike anything here on earth.

非欧几里得球体，与地球上的任何事物都截然不同。

Loathsomely redolent dimensions completely unlike ours.

令人作呕的、散发着异域风情的维度，与我们的世界截然不同。

Now a seaman was describing the exact same thing.

现在，一名水手描述的也是同样的事情。

They bad both had the same terrible glimpse of this reality.

他们都曾目睹过这种可怕的现实。

Johansen and his men landed at a sloping mud-bank.

约翰森和他的部下在倾斜的泥滩上登陆。

And they looked up at this monstrous Acropolis.

他们抬头望向这座巍峨的卫城。

They clambered slippery up over titan oozy blocks.

他们小心翼翼地爬过巨大的、黏糊糊的方块。

Blocks which could have been no mortal staircase.

这些方块原本不可能是凡人所能建造的楼梯。

The very sun of heaven seemed distorted in this mist.

就连天上的太阳似乎也在这片迷雾中扭曲变形了。

A polarizing miasma welling out from this sea-soaked perversion.

从这片浸透海水的扭曲之地涌现出一股两极分化的迷雾。

Twisted menace and suspense lurked in those elusive rocks.

那些神秘莫测的岩石中潜藏着扭曲的威胁和悬念。

A second glance showed concavity where the first showed convexity.

第二眼看去，第一眼看到的是凸面，第二眼看到的却是凹面。

Something very like fright had come over all the explorers.

所有探险家都感到一阵莫名的恐惧。

Each man would have fled had he not feared the scorn of the others.

如果不是害怕其他人的嘲笑，他们每个人都会逃走。

And it was only half-heartedly that they vainly searched.

他们只是漫不经心地徒劳地寻找着。

They were looking for some portable souvenir to bear away.

他们想找一些可以带走的便携式纪念品。

It was Rodriguez, the Portuguese, who climbed up the foot of the monolith.

是葡萄牙人罗德里格斯爬上了巨石的底部。

From there he shouted of what he had found.

他从那里大声喊出他发现的东西。

The rest followed him to the foot of the monolith.

其余的人跟着他来到巨石脚下。

They looked curiously at the immense door in front of them.

他们好奇地看着眼前这扇巨大的门。

The now familiar squid-dragon was carved on the door.

门上雕刻着我们现在熟悉的鱿鱼龙图案。

It was, Johansen said, like a great barn-door.

约翰森说，那就像一扇巨大的谷仓门。

Although they said it only gave the impression of a door.

虽然他们说它只是给人一种门的错觉。

They could not decide if the door lay flat like a trap-door.

他们无法确定这扇门是否像活板门一样平放。

Or maybe the opening was slanted like an outside cellar-door.

或许开口是倾斜的，就像地窖的外门一样。

As Wilcox would have said, the geometry of the place was all wrong.

正如威尔科克斯会说的那样，这个地方的几何结构完全不对。

One could not be sure that the sea and the ground were horizontal.

人们无法确定大海和陆地是否水平。

Hence the relative position of everything else seemed phantasmally variable.

因此，其他一切事物的相对位置似乎都变得异常多变。

Briden pushed at the stone in several places, without result.

布里登多次推搡石头，但都没有效果。

Then Donovan felt delicately over around the edge of the door.

然后多诺万小心翼翼地摸到了门边。

He climbed interminably along the grotesque stone molding.

他沿着怪诞的石雕线条没完没了地攀爬。

Although, if you could really call it climbing is debatable.

不过，这是否真的能称之为攀岩还有待商榷。

Perhaps the door was more horizontal than vertical.

或许这扇门与其说是竖直的，不如说是水平的。

And the men wondered how any door in the universe could be so vast.

男人们不禁疑惑，宇宙中怎么可能有如此巨大的门。

Then, very softly and slowly, something began to happen.

然后，非常轻柔、缓慢地，一些事情开始发生了。

The acre-great panel began to give inward at the top.

这块巨大的面板顶部开始向内凹陷。

And they saw that the door had balanced itself.

他们发现门已经自行保持平衡了。

***

Donovan somehow propelled himself back along the jamb.

多诺万不知怎么地沿着门框向后挪了挪。

And everyone watched the queer recession of the monstrously carven portal.

所有人都目睹了这座造型怪异的门户的奇异衰退。

In this fantasy of prismatic distortion it moved anomalously in a diagonal way.

在这种棱镜扭曲的幻想中，它以异常的对角线方式移动。

All the rules of matter and perspective seemed confused.

物质和透视的所有规则似乎都变得混乱了。

The aperture was black with a darkness almost material.

孔径呈黑色，仿佛覆盖着一层黑暗的物质。

That tenebrousness was indeed a positive quality.

这种阴暗的氛围实际上是一种积极的特质。

The men were spared from seeing the inner walls.

这些人免于看到内墙。

The darkness burst forth like smoke from its eon-long imprisonment.

黑暗如同烟雾般从漫长的囚禁中喷涌而出。

The sun was visibly darkened by flapping membranous wings.

拍打着膜状翅膀，太阳明显被遮蔽了。

And the shadow slunk away into the shrunken and gibbous sky.

阴影悄然消失在缩小而凸起的天空中。

The odor arising from the newly opened depths was intolerable.

从新开启的深处散发出的气味令人难以忍受。

The quick-eared Hawkins thought he heard a nasty, slopping sound.

耳朵灵敏的霍金斯似乎听到了一种难听的、哗哗作响的声音。

His ears were confirmed when It lumbered slobberingly into sight.

当它笨拙地、流着口水地出现在视线中时，他的耳朵得到了证实。

Its gelatinous green immensity groped through the black hall.

它那胶状的绿色庞然大物在漆黑的大厅里摸索着。

And Its ooze and smell squeezed through the angled door.

它的黏液和气味从倾斜的门缝里挤了出来。

The Thing went into the tainted air of that poison city of madness.

那东西进入了那座疯狂毒城的污浊空气中。

Poor Johansen's handwriting almost gave out when he wrote of this.

可怜的约翰森在写下这段文字时，字迹几乎都写不出来。

He thinks two men perished of pure fright in that accursed instant.

他认为在那该死的瞬间，有两个人因极度恐惧而丧命。

The Thing cannot be described with our language.

这种东西无法用我们的语言来描述。

There are no words for such abysms of shrieking and immemorial lunacy.

如此深渊般的尖叫和亘古不变的疯狂，简直无法用语言来形容。

Eldritch contradictions of all matter, force, and cosmic order.

物质、力量和宇宙秩序中存在的诡异矛盾。

A mountain that walked and stumbled on the earth. God!

一座行走于大地之上，跌跌撞撞的山。上帝啊！

No wonder that across the earth a great architect went mad.

难怪地球上一位伟大的建筑师会发疯。

No wonder poor Wilcox raved with fever in that telepathic instant.

难怪可怜的威尔科克斯在那瞬间心灵感应时会发高烧，语无伦次。

The green, sticky spawn of the stars, was walking the earth.

这些绿色、黏糊糊的星际生物，正在地球上行走。

The Thing of the idols had awaked to claim his own.

偶像之物苏醒了，要夺回属于自己的领地。

The stars were aligned again, as was predicted.

正如预言的那样，星辰再次排列成一条直线。

An age-old cult had failed in their duties.

一个古老的邪教组织未能履行其职责。

And a band of innocent sailors fulfilled their role by accident.

一群无辜的水手无意中完成了他们的任务。

After vigintillions of years great Cthulhu was loose again.

经过亿万年之后，伟大的克苏鲁再次重获自由。

And now great Cthulhu was ravening for delight.

而现在，伟大的克苏鲁正渴望着极致的欢愉。

Three men were swept up by the flabby claws before anybody turned.

还没等任何人回头，三个男人就被那双肥爪子卷走了。

God rest them, if there be any rest in the universe.

愿上帝安息他们，如果宇宙间真有安息之所的话。

Let it be known that their names were Donovan, Guerrera and Angstrom.

特此声明，他们的名字分别是多诺万、格雷拉和安格斯特罗姆。

Parker slipped as he was trying to make his escape.

帕克在逃跑时滑倒了。

The other three were plunging frenziedly back to the boat.

另外三人拼命地往船上跳。

They ran over endless vistas of green-crusted rock.

他们奔跑在无尽的绿色岩壳之上。

Johansen swears he was swallowed up by an angle of masonry.

约翰森发誓说他被一块砖石的棱角吞没了。

An angle which shouldn't have been there.

一个不该出现在那里的角度。

An angle which was acute, but behaved as if it were obtuse.

一个锐角，但表现得像钝角一样。

Only Briden and Johansen made it back to the boat.

只有布里登和约翰森回到了船上。

The two men had a moment of good fortune.

两人都走了运。

The mountainous monstrosity flopped down on the slimy stones.

那座山峦般的庞然大物重重地摔在了湿滑的石头上。

And the beast hesitated floundering at the edge of the water.

那野兽在水边犹豫不决，挣扎着。

The steam boat had not entirely run out of hot coals.

汽船上的热煤还没有完全用完。

Despite the departure of all men for the shore.

尽管所有男人都已前往岸边。

Feverishly the two men rushed up and down between wheels.

两人慌慌张张地在车轮间上上下下地奔跑。

It was the work of only a few moments to get the engine going.

启动引擎只用了很短的时间。

Amidst the distorted horrors of that indescribable scene.

在那难以描述的恐怖场景中。

Slowly their boat began to churn the lethal waters beneath her.

他们的船开始缓缓搅动船底致命的海水。

And they moved along the masonry of that charnel shore.

他们沿着那片尸骸遍野的海岸的石砌路面前进。

That strange coastline that was not from this world.

那片奇异的海岸线，仿佛不属于这个世界。

***

The titan Thing from the stars slavered and gibbered.

来自星际的巨型怪物流着口水，胡言乱语。

Like Polypheme cursing the fleeing ship of Odysseus.

就像波吕斐摩斯诅咒奥德修斯逃亡的船只一样。

Then great Cthulhu slid greasily into the water.

然后，巨大的克苏鲁滑入了水中。

Bolder and more daring than the storied Cyclops.

比传说中的独眼巨人更大胆、更无畏。

Cthulhu pursued them through the water with cosmic movement.

克苏鲁以宇宙般的速度在水中追逐着他们。

Briden looked back from the ship and started laughing shrilly.

布里登从船上回头望去，开始发出尖锐的笑声。

From that moment Briden continued laughing at odd intervals.

从那一刻起，布里登不时地发出笑声。

But Johansen had not given up yet.

但约翰森还没有放弃。

He knew his ship had no chance of outpacing the thing.

他知道自己的船根本不可能跑赢那东西。

So he resolved on taking a desperate chance.

于是他决定孤注一掷。

He loaded the furnace and set the engine for full speed.

他给炉子装好燃料，并将发动机调到全速运转。

And then he ran lightning-like on deck and reversed the wheel.

然后他像闪电一样跑到甲板上，反转了方向盘。

There was a mighty eddying and foaming in the noisome brine.

刺鼻的盐水中翻腾起巨大的漩涡和泡沫。

The steam mounted higher and higher into the sky.

蒸汽越升越高，直冲云霄。

And the brave Norwegian reversed the course of the chase.

勇敢的挪威人扭转了追逐的局面。

Before him rose the unclean froth like the stern of a demon galleon.

在他面前升起污浊的泡沫，如同恶魔战船的船尾。

He drove his vessel head on against the pursuing jelly.

他驾驶着船头直冲着追赶他的水母而去。

The awful squid-head came nearly up to the yacht's bowsprit.

那可怕的鱿鱼头几乎爬到了游艇的船首斜桅上。

But Johansen drove on relentlessly against the writhing feelers.

但约翰森毫不气馁，继续逆着蠕动的触须前进。

There was a bursting as of an exploding bladder.

传来一声爆裂声，就像膀胱爆炸一样。

There was a slushy nastiness as of a cloven sunfish.

那里有一种像翻车鱼一样黏糊糊的恶心感。

There was a stench as of a thousand opened graves.

空气中弥漫着一股如同上千个坟墓被打开般的恶臭。

And there was a sound the chronicler did not put on paper.

还有一种声音，编年史家没有记录下来。

For an instant the ship was befouled by an acrid cloud.

一瞬间，船身被一股刺鼻的气味笼罩。

The green cloud blinded Johansen and the mad man.

绿色的云雾遮蔽了约翰森和那个疯子的眼睛。

And then there was only a venomous seething astern.

然后，只剩下充满毒性的沸腾船尾。

But God in heaven! What the two men saw next;

但是，我的天哪！接下来这两个人看到了什么？

The scattered plasticity of that nameless sky-spawn.

那无名天降生物的零散可塑性。

The injured thing was nebulously recombining.

受伤的物体正在模糊地重组。

Soon Cthulhu would be back in its hateful original form.

不久之后，克苏鲁就会以其令人憎恶的原始形态回归。

But their distance was widening with every second.

但他们之间的距离却每秒都在拉大。

The ship was gaining impetus from its mounting steam.

船只凭借不断增强的蒸汽获得了更大的动力。

And eventually the cursed city was over the horizon.

最终，那座被诅咒的城市出现在了地平线上。

***

He did not try to navigate after their lucky escape.

他们侥幸逃脱后，他并没有尝试导航。

His reaction had taken something out of his soul.

他的反应仿佛抽走了他灵魂的一部分。

He spent his time brooding over the idol in the cabin.

他整天待在小屋里，对着偶像沉思。

He looked after the laughing maniac in the boat.

他照顾了船上那个大笑的疯子。

And he attended to a few matters such as food.

他还处理了一些其他事务，比如食物。

Then came the storm of April 2nd.

然后，4月2日那场暴风雨来了。

On that day clouds gathered over his consciousness.

那天，他的思绪仿佛被乌云笼罩。

There is a sense of pure and refined delirium.

有一种纯粹而精致的迷醉感。

Spectral whirling through liquid gulfs of infinity.

幽灵般的漩涡在无垠的液态深渊中旋转。

Dizzying rides through reeling universes on a comet's tail.

乘坐彗星尾巴，在令人眼花缭乱的宇宙中穿梭。

Hysterical plunges from the pit to the moon.

从深渊到月球的歇斯底里式坠落。

And he plunged back again from the moon to the pit.

于是他又从月球坠落回了深渊。

A cachinnating chorus of the distorted, hilarious elder gods.

一群滑稽可笑、扭曲怪诞的远古神灵发出令人捧腹的合唱。

And the green bat-winged mocking imps of Tartarus.

还有塔尔塔罗斯那些长着绿色蝙蝠翅膀的嘲讽小恶魔。

Out of that dream came rescue; the ship Vigilant.

从那个梦境中，救援出现了；那就是"警戒号"飞船。

The vice-admiralty court and the streets of Dunedin.

海军副司令法庭和达尼丁的街道。

The long voyage back home to the old house by the Egeberg.

漫长的返乡之旅，回到埃格贝格山边的老房子。

He could not tell anyone of what he had seen.

他无法将自己所看到的一切告诉任何人。

Had he told the truth they would have thought he had gone mad.

如果他说了实话，他们会认为他疯了。

So he secretly wrote of what he knew before death came.

所以，在临终前，他秘密地写下了他所知道的一切。

"Death would be a boon if only it could blot out the memories."

"如果死亡能够抹去记忆，那将是一件好事。"

That was the document Johansen left behind.

那是约翰森留下的文件。

And now I have placed this document in the tin box.

现在我已经把这份文件放进了铁盒里。

In the box is also the dream carved bas-relief.

盒子里还有一幅雕刻着梦境的浅浮雕。

And I have included the papers of Professor Angell.

我还收录了安吉尔教授的论文。

With this box shall go this record of mine.

我的这张唱片将随这个盒子一起存放。

These notes have become a test of my own sanity.

这些笔记成了对我自身理智的考验。

But I hope my discoveries are never be pieced together again.

但我希望我的发现永远不会再次被拼凑起来。

I have looked upon all that the universe has to hold of horror.

我已目睹宇宙间所有恐怖之物。

But now even the skies of spring are darkness to me.

但现在，就连春天的天空对我来说也变成了黑暗。

Even the flowers of summer are forever poison to me.

就连夏天的花朵对我来说也永远是毒药。

But I do not think my life will be long.

但我认为我的寿命不会很长。

As my uncle went, so shall my end come.

叔叔走了，我的结局也将如此。

As poor Johansen went, so shall my time come.

可怜的约翰森就这样走了，我的末日也终将到来。

I know too much, and the cult still lives.

我知道得太多了，而邪教依然存在。

Cthulhu still lives, too, I can only suppose.

我只能推测，克苏鲁也还活着。

I assume Cthulhu is again in that chasm of stone.

我猜想克苏鲁又被困在那道石窟里了。

The city which has shielded him since the sun was young.

这座城市自太阳诞生之初就一直庇护着他。

I know his accursed city is sunken once more.

我知道他那座被诅咒的城市再次沉没了。

The crew of the Vigilant sailed over the spot after the April storm.

四月风暴过后，"警戒号"的船员驶过该地点。

But his ministers on earth still worship his return.

但他在世上的信徒仍然崇拜他的再来。

In lonely places they congregate around their idol.

在人迹罕至的地方，他们会聚集在偶像周围。

And they bellow and prance and slay in satanic ritual.

他们咆哮、跳跃、杀戮，进行着撒旦式的仪式。

He must have been trapped by the sinking of his black abyss.

他一定是陷入了黑色深渊的沉没之中。

Or else the world would by now be screaming with fright and frenzy.

否则，世界现在应该已经陷入恐慌和疯狂之中了。

Who knows how the end will come about?

谁知道结局会如何呢？

What has risen may sink, and what has sunk may rise.

上升的事物可能会沉没，沉没的事物可能会上升。

Loathsomeness waits and dreams in the deep.

令人厌恶的事物在深处潜伏和盘旋。

And decay spreads over the tottering cities of men.

腐朽蔓延至摇摇欲坠的人类城市。

A time will come where that city rises out the sea again.

总有一天，那座城市会再次从海中升起。

But I must not think about when that day will come!

但我不能去想那一天何时到来！

I have one prayer if this manuscript outlives me.

如果这份手稿能比我活得更久，我只有一个愿望。

I pray my executors put caution before audacity.

我祈祷我的遗嘱执行人能够谨慎行事，而不是鲁莽行事。

I pray this manuscript meets no other eyes.

我祈祷这份手稿不会落入他人之手。

***

Found among the papers of the late Francis Wayland Thurston, of Boston.

在已故波士顿人弗朗西斯·韦兰·瑟斯顿的遗物中发现。